WELCOME TO HEIDI

WELCOME TO HEIDI

HEIDI CLEMENTS

Published 2014 by HumorOutcasts Press
Printed in the United States of America

ISBN 0-692-21684-7
EAN-13 978-069221684-2

Cover Photo Mark Steines
Cover Design by Erik Photenhauer

DEDICATION

To everyone who's ever made me feel like my dreams don't matter. You inspire me to defy you. Oh and you were wrong. I win.

ACKNOWLEDGMENTS

Thank you to my friends, my family and the total strangers who encourage me to write what I feel and feel safe doing it.

To Donna Cavanagh and Julie Ross for physically making this book come to life and Bruce Ferber for pointing the way to these women.

Introduction

In the pantheon of serious American feminist thinkers and writers of the 20th century, you will not find the name Heidi Clements. That's because she wrote this book in 2014, and she's actually funny. In fact, this hilarious post, post, post-feminist collection of stories should be required reading for any modern woman, and for men who love women, men who love women but have sex with other men, and men who want to become women, and vice-versa. Because man or woman, deep down in all of us, there's a brilliant Jewish woman shaking her fist at an unfair world. In "Welcome to Heidi," Clements is a funnier, more biting Carrie Bradshaw with even better shoes and minus the cloying insecurity. When "having it all" was once the post-feminist mantra, Clements wants only one thing: to be unapologetically herself. These are her stories -- about a woman's hilarious and fierce, unencumbered pursuit to be self-realized, defined by no one, guided by a stringent no-assholes policy, two French mastiffs and a Chihuahua.

Brian Unger, Journalist, Actor, Television Host, and all around Amazing, Hilarious and Very Hot Human Being (Heidi wrote this part)

Chapter One

Happy Birthday to Mean

"Let's face it. You're on the downside of life now," a friend said to me on my 50th birthday. "You're basically just careening to the end." I stabbed him with a fork. Then I went out and bought some new shoes.

If you're one of those women prancing around shouting that 50 is the new 30, then you need to cut back on the scotch. The only thing 50 is – is 50. If you're lucky, you're halfway through your life. If you're not – well, you may keel over halfway through this book.

There is a kind of wisdom you get when you hit 40 – this amazing and enlightening invisible book you're handed that has all the answers to the questions you've been pondering for four decades. You find yourself walking around talking to yourself going, "Ohhhhhhhh, now I get it. Gosh, if only I'd known that when I was 20." Blah. Blah. Whatever. That's the genius of youth – even if you have any kind of knowledge, you don't want to use it. It's annoying. Logic is kryptonite to young people. They back away from it like the liquor-free punch bowl at a frat party. No one wants it. They can be smart later in life. Who needs brains when there is a bong and you have an Instagram account to document your stupidity?

Forty can be troubling, but I highly recommend marking the occasion. Just don't quit drinking four months before your 40th, then throw a party and invite all your boozy friends whom you secretly curse, and call "liquor pigs," and hate because they're drunk on your birthday, and everything they say is stupid, and you're not drunk because you're a loser who couldn't handle your alcohol. Also, try not to take a baseball bat to a piñata that the neighbors you don't even know (and occasionally make fun of because they're weird) got you for your birthday, and eat a ton of sheet cake before crying alone in your bedroom at 2 am, and then eat the rest of the cake out of the garbage with a fork. It could happen.

But 40 is deal-able. The only thing I got when I turned 50 was meaner – and I was pretty cranky to begin with. I immediately started to think about death all the time. I found myself talking to God, asking to be spared as if there was a plague on the way sweeping up all the 50-year-olds. Somehow I became Cloris Leachman overnight. My boobs moved to their final resting place – which, sadly, was my waist. Being able to tuck your breasts into your pants is not something to celebrate. It is also, not sexy. Suddenly everything I did hurt, and by everything I mean bending over to tie my shoe. Is this how it happens? You turn 50 and the people upstairs go, "Oh, there she is – zap her. Turn her life upside down. Make her old." I mean, I know age is just a number, but suddenly my number was really old. *Will I be getting that weird back hump soon? Do I have to start eating dinner at 5:30 now? Will I be allowed a later reservation? When do I start saying, "This music's too loud"? Wait – I say that now.*

I was never a huge fan of people, but now I hated everyone who didn't think exactly like me, and I was driven into a homicidal-type rage by even the simplest of things. *Why is everyone so stupid?* I'd sit in my car and curse at people at traffic lights who paused for a split second when it went from red to green. "What are you waiting for?" I'd scream like a mental patient. The bigger question was – What am I in such a rush to get to? The supermarket, where there were more stupid people waiting to piss me off? I am constantly standing behind the person who says, "Oh, I forgot something. I'll be right back." *Great. I'll just wait here for you to run through the entire store like it's the game show "Supermarket Sweep" and see if you can find the can of lima beans you can't live without but couldn't remember to pick up while you were shoving the Double Stuff Oreos and other carcinogenic crap into your cart, you giant Nut Bag. And by the way you're too fat to eat those cookies. Breathe, Heidi. Just breathe.*

The second I hit 50, all of the ads on television were about me and the terrible, horrible, disturbing things that were going to happen to my body. Did you know that your pelvic floor is going to drop, and you'll need to exercise it? Did you know your pelvis had a floor? I didn't. (I hope mine's a dance floor.) My mom called and told me she had to have an operation on her lady parts and their surroundings because– quote – everything dropped. Perfect. That sounds fun. I guess your insides don't want to feel left out that your outsides need to be lifted, so the whole system just crashes to the ground.

And she wasn't the only mother with bad news. My friend Becky's mom, Leslie, sent me a catalog called "As We Change." She thought I would find it funny. I was rocked into a depression that sent me directly to sugar-filled items. I found out I'm going to need things that I was not expecting to need – like a pillow to shove down my bra while I sleep to keep me from getting creases in my chest. (P.S. This one's too late.) There are at least three pairs of gloves I'm going to have to buy for various stages of achiness in my wrists, fingers, and palms. I will need to restore my hair to its youthful fullness, and if I can't, there's a spray that I can use to paint my head. There are creams for my soon-to-be-blotchy skin, tapes to remove my brow wrinkles, and balms to smooth out the lines around my lips. There are pills to stop my nails from breaking, bleaches to stop my face from darkening, and oils to re-lube what's un-lube able. Fuck. I'm going to be a hot mess.

I think the most disturbing items in the catalog were the clothing, shoes, and handbags – which were really brightly colored and covered in things like butterflies and waves. I have never owned one thing with a butterfly on it, and if you see me in something that does, please call someone and report it immediately. Then have me killed. I don't know who you call for stuff like this, but if you love me – you'll research that and get it done. *When does this overwhelming need to wear hideous clothing begin? Does it suddenly become acceptable to carry a quilted bag? When do I start wearing Mom Jeans? Do they just come in the mail, or do I have to order them? When do I cut off all of my hair and layer on the chunky jewelry?*

There were some strappy sandals in the catalog that I wouldn't be caught dead in – even if I were dead. There was something called a "Boob Tube" to wear under lower-cut dresses and tops, because apparently no one wants to see old woman cleavage. (I know I don't.) There were comfy straps to put under my bra straps to cut down on "unsightly dents" – which is another way of saying your giant Old Woman Boobs are dropping at such a rapid rate, the stress on your shoulders is leaving a mark in your skin that is not sexy. Color me terrific. There were foam nipple covers (no idea why), instant buttons to expand your pants (could be using those right now), and shoe stretchers to help shove your swollen lumps into your Christian Louboutins. (*Shit, when do I have to give my high heels back because I can't walk in them anymore? Add that to the list of things that suck it when you get old.*) There was even a special necklace you can slip your no-longer-fits-your-fat- fingers wedding band onto. (*Well, there's one thing I don't need. Thank goodness I didn't get married. Am I right or am I right?*)

There were heel-huggers, and toe-compressors, and bunion-smoothers, and 66 pages of magical Old People Shit, and I haven't even read the section on bathing suits because I'm quite certain I could buy every single one of them right now. When it comes with a slimming panel, a high neck, silicone shapers, a skirt, a built-in diaper, and a matching sarong, I say, "Why wait? Let's get this party started."

I wonder if there's one of these catalogs for men. It's probably the exact same catalog, but it's called "As She Changes," and it's just there to inform men of all the things they shouldn't bring up so they don't send us into an endless hormonal crying jag. Men don't need a catalog of all the stuff that's going to fall apart on them, because they don't care. As long as the penis stays attached – they're good to go. I, on the other hand, just ordered a bra wash bag and some Goodnighties Recovery Sleepwear infused with negative ions to help me sleep. Hey, if it's good enough for astronauts – it's good enough for this old broad.

I used to think the biggest concern for me was the rapid rate at which my hair was graying. I now need to have my naturally red hair dyed every three weeks, and by natural, I mean I pay for it, so shut the fuck up. But just yesterday while I was at the salon, I noticed an elderly woman having her gray hair dyed to an incredibly unbelievable shade of some sort of brown that was not on any Pantene dye wheel I've ever seen. She looked like a doll - a really old doll. I wanted to tell her that it was time to just say "yes" to the gray and "no" to the helmet of henna tint she was sporting, but I was too overwhelmed by another part of her anatomy – her ear lobes. They were huge and swingy and clearly not the lobes she came into this life with. In fact, just one quick glimpse of these fleshy flops and I knew – they had grown, and someday, so would mine. I immediately Googled, "Do ear lobes grow as we get older?" and bam - yes, they do. Great. Something else to look forward to. My ear lobes will drop down to where my boobs, ass, and knees are all gathering. Eventually, won't I just be a head with pudding skin all piled around down by my ankles? There isn't enough industrial-strength tape to pull it all back up.

I'm already obsessed with grabbing the skin on the back of my neck and then crying when I release it. I worked with Jane Seymour once, and she used Scotch tape on the back of hers. I watched her do it. It was remarkable. The company should totally add this to their advertising campaign. That shit is strong. *Why do my ear lobes have to grow? Who do I call to skip this part? Is there some sort of list I can check where I get to pick just three of the gazillion hideous things that are happening to my body? Something like:*

1. Boob hair – No, thank you.

2. Nose hair – Not really interested.

3. Ear hair – Shut the fuck up.

4. Saggy boobs – Fine, if I have to.

5. Cellulite – Okay, I can undress alone.

6. Leaky vagina – Don't really want to smell like pee yet.

7. Wrinkles – Whatever.

8. Menopause – Can't wait.

9. Crepe-y Skin – Fine.

10. Grey Hair – Sure.

I could go on, but I just depressed myself. It's already crystal-clear that I'm becoming completely invisible to the opposite sex. Just yesterday, I lost the "final frontier" of feeling pretty – the inside of my car. Until recently, when I got dolled up and drove somewhere, I could get at least get one look from a man in a passing car. You can't tell what I look like from the neck down, and my hair can block a whole lot of issues. But yesterday, on my way to a party, I got nothing. Zero. Zip. Loser. Old Lady. Set yourself on fire, and maybe someone will turn their head in your direction. It's over, people. Now I'm just waiting for my lobes to grow so I have somewhere to hang the "out of business" sign.

Everything seems to be going at once. My eyesight is a shit storm. I cursed out my optometrist because I couldn't read anything with my new contact lenses in. He then informed me that I needed reading glasses. I already have terrible distance vision. Basically, I'm like – blind. I can't get out of bed without putting glasses on, because I will surely fall down. Sometimes, I wake up in the middle of the night with an idea, and I email it to myself so I don't forget it by morning. This is what I emailed myself last night: "My do tlip nods khedive needs breTh rifhbr strips." If anyone knows what that means, please call me. People tell me to get that Lasik eye surgery all the time, but I'm not having my corneas slashed to ribbons with a laser beam by a guy who advertises during "Bad Girls" on Oxygen. What if we find out that 20 years after you have Lasik surgery, your entire head falls off? Who cares how clear your vision is then?

I hate having to wear reading glasses. It immediately makes you feel 100 years old. I have a friend who's so freaked out about having to wear reading glasses that she goes to what I would call extremes to avoid revealing her blurry little secret – and you have to go pretty far for me to call it extreme. If she has a date, she has her assistant call the restaurant so they can fax the menu to her home. Then – like a high school girl cramming for a calculus test – she memorizes it. Do the math. This is nuts. She also calls the restaurant on her way there to make sure they haven't added anything to the menu at the last minute – like fried boar. Because in her mind, it would be a clear sign something was amiss if she didn't say, "How unusual that they serve fried boar here, no?" Trust me: If a woman wears reading glasses on a date, no man will care. As long as her vagina can see his penis, he'll be good to go.

Turning 50 is both a gift and a curse. You really do become a completely filter-free version of yourself, and you finally understand that you have to be asked for advice and not just throw your opinion at people. I think the,"I know what I'm talking about, you moron" speech comes at about 60, and I'm not gonna lie, I look forward to that. I can feel it gently tickling the back of my neck. The hardest part of turning 50 is understanding that sexually, it's over. And I know what all you sexually active women are saying right now: "That's not me. I'm banging around like a kid." Well, good for you. I'll call the Old People Porn Channel and tell them you're making a hot new video. But I am fairly convinced that no guy wakes up in the morning and says, "I need to find a hot 50-year-old broad to punch in the pants today." If he does, please give him my address, phone number, and email.

There are also great things about turning the Big Five-O. You really know who you are, and if you're lucky, you're happy with that person. You stop wasting time with toxic people, and you don't let yourself get undermined by the insanity of others. You're fine if you don't get invited to every party, and staying home on the couch at night in your underpants with an array of snack items that could kill you is better than an invitation to the Oscars. Those beautiful people don't talk to we great unwashed anyway.

I think the one thing I finally realized when I turned 50 was who the great love of my life is – me. I have learned to love myself, and when necessary, laugh at myself. I have also learned that your life is like a movie, and if you don't like the way it's playing – rewrite it and recast it. I did. I quit my six-figure job and took a long hard look at my life. Then I threw up. Then I got some new shoes. Happy birthday to me.

Chapter Two

The Devil Wears LuLu Lemon

I had to quit my job because I was being ass-raped on a daily basis by a big blonde bully. Verbally only, but it still hurt. Yes, I was run right out of the Valley by a fifty-something-year-old plastic surgery addict who was so overcome with her jealousy of me that she went mental, and then she tried to take me down the rabbit hole with her. It happened slowly, creeping up on me like a cancer over the course of seven years. And while I didn't lose my hair, I did get some lovely and very expensive parting gifts.

I remember the very carefully chosen words of advice my friend gave me on my first day at work with the soul-crusher: "Don't talk to her. Do not engage. In fact, try not to look her in the eye at all." (Yes, people really do say that in Hollywood.) This is not an easy assignment when you work on a television show run by a peroxide-blonde dictator who expects people to quit their lives when they start working for her but hey – I was willing to give it the old college try. I had incentive. I was broke and was starting to get really scared I'd be living in a box next to my friend John, who is homeless and has no teeth, but a lovely smile.

The first thing I did was completely ignore my friend's advice. This whirling dervish was intriguing to me – like a wild animal roaming the halls of an office. I wanted to get close enough to pet it and see what would happen. I couldn't resist. I did a bad thing. I engaged – and then I tickled the tiger – just for fun.

Every day at work was an adventure in insanity. If a celebrity news story broke, she went into happy overdrive, and if that story was something horrible happening to that certain celebrity – her glee was mind numbing. We'd all look at each other wondering, *"Is this really happening? Did she just say that?"* I'm not sure – but I think I once saw foam come out of her mouth. The second a star story would cross the wires we'd all cringe, knowing what was about to happen. As if an air raid siren was going off, our first instincts were to duck under our desks – but we had to spring to action. If you didn't follow orders, you'd be singled out – and the wrath was terrifying. Her favorite word was "chaos," and if there wasn't any happening around her, she would create it. She loved this. If it was a nice quiet day in the newsroom, then something was terribly wrong. She adored watching people spin themselves out of control to get whatever she wanted – and the request could be anything from a helicopter to fried chicken. Though she usually wanted fried chicken. I eventually changed her ring tone on my phone to an air raid siren so I knew when she was calling. It was both hilarious and cold sweat inducing.

She actually loved to scream and yell at people, and the bigger the crowd that was watching – the better. You could see how the anger fueled her, her decibel level growing louder the more terrified the employee became. She thrived on the sound of her own voice, and once she started blasting, she couldn't stop and would whip herself into such a frenzy that her face would turn bright red and her eyes would widen. You knew you were staring into the face of the devil, and her pitchfork was her tongue jabbing you until you bled. Emotionally. The only weird part was, she was always smiling during these moments – grinning from ear to ear like the Joker. I'm pretty sure this was the result of a shit-ton of plastic surgery and Botox needles, because her face was frozen into some kind of twisted smile that made it hard to tell if she was truly angry. But she was. Angry was her favorite place to be. I would stare at her while she was screaming at me and think – *"Why is she smiling?"* There was even an office she gleefully called "The Crying Room" where she sent any employee that needed a good cry because no one should cry in the open at the office – especially since she was the one inducing most of the tears.

But like I said – there was a price for being on the end of her ear-splitting rants – gifts. Very expensive gifts. I got two Chanel handbags and a Louis Vuitton suitcase. Blood luggage, I call it. But I use it. I earned it. Everyone knew that if she went off on you – you got a gift. Like the white angry Oprah, she should have raced through the office yelling, "You get Chanel! You get Chanel!"

She liked to think she was a free-spirited thinker who nurtured her employees with her warm and fuzzy style. She was, in fact, about as warm and fuzzy as a porcupine popsicle, and if the words "you're an idiot" are nurturing, well then, she was indeed an ego-builder. She loved when employees called her "Mommy." But if you made "Mommy" mad – you got a lot more than a time out. If she was $1 over budget, she would fire anyone in sight – well, not her sight, because she made sure to be on vacation when the hammer came down. That was someone else's job. I'll call him Henry. And he eventually saved my ass.

I remember the first time she decided I should be the one to fire someone. She actually gave me two names and made me pick between them. I think she even referred to it as my "Sophie's Choice." Now, no one was going to a death camp, but she was certainly killing their chances of providing for their wives and children. This did not faze her. She would have gladly bought them some train tickets and threw in a few pairs of striped pajamas if it meant her precious budget would be back on track.

She would never explain what had happened to fired employees – they would just disappear – perhaps picked up and taken in for anal probes on the Alien Mother Ship. I have no problem with people losing their jobs because they aren't good at them – but our people were fired because she had spent too much money buying videotapes of stars doing bad things – except our star – who was caught making some very dirty and very funny audiotapes. He got a one-hour special on a talk show and a stint or two in rehab.

One of the things my boss really didn't like was anyone else's ideas if they were better than hers, which they inevitably were because her ideas stopped popping into her head around 1982. She loved Donny and Marie, Barry Manilow, and the Royal Family. I once told her that the only time we should put Barry on again is when he came out of the closet. I might as well have raped her dog. She was horrified by this suggestion. To her, Barry Manilow was at the peak of his career. He was not.

Over the course of my stint there, I kept getting promoted and eventually landed in the catbird seat as her

Number Two – an appropriate title considering how she made me feel on a daily basis. She was constantly threatening to demote me. I remember the day some network bigwigs were coming in for a meeting. She ordered me to get my hair and makeup done. I said I was fine without it. She then screamed at me. I continued to object. She turned to me with that creepy tight-lipped smile and whispered through clenched teeth, "Why do you always have to argue with me?" I got the hair and makeup. The meeting went smoothly, and I tried to be my bubbly self. But moments after the bigwigs left, she turned to me and said, "Please don't have an opinion that's different from mine in front of other people."

I actually thought she was right for about a nanosecond, but I was smack in the midst of my Anne Frank years at this job, where my real personality was trapped in an attic scribbling in dirty notebooks. Most people who came to work there ended up drinking the Kool-Aid and settling in for a nice long bout of Stockholm Syndrome. This bitch was scary. People were terrified of her. I became one of those people.

She was obsessed with the talents' wardrobes and only wanted our reporters in bright, solid-color dresses. She liked everyone to look like a bag of Skittles or Teletubbies. On the day of the Met Costume Ball in New York City, I found out just how much this meant to her. Our offices were in California, so thanks to the time difference, the people in New York were left up to their own devices for the most part. The only problem was – shooting something the boss hadn't approved literally became a crapshoot. There we were, watching the footage that had been shot earlier feed in on the satellite. Tons of gorgeous stars in beautiful gowns walked before our cameras, and then boom! Her face turned red. Her voice hit a new level of loud. "What the hell is she wearing?" she screamed at the top of her lungs as our talent appeared before the camera to do her stand-up. We all looked at the monitor and saw that our stunningly beautiful reporter had committed the most heinous of sins – she was wearing BEIGE. "Get her on the phone for me now!" We all watched in fear and horror as she shredded this grown woman over the phone. "Beige? How could you wear beige?! No one will see you in beige! If the golden arches were beige, no one would eat there." When the reporter answered, "But Gucci made it." the boss replied, "I don't care if Jesus made it."

Over the course of my seven years there, she made some truly standout statements. I wish I'd written more of them down, but I was far too busy being shocked and awed. Some of my favorites were, "Does anyone remember if I took my pills today?" (she took a lot) and (when showing her surgery scars to an employee who winced) "You've been through childbirth – buck the fuck up." She told our African American reporter that he couldn't be the anchor because America wasn't ready for a black host. She also asked an employee who had happily announced her pregnancy if she wanted a ride to the abortion clinic. She is not a fan of worker bees having kids. That kind of cuts in to your 24-hour devotion to the all-important culling of negative celebrity news no one needs to hear.

She also did some fairly insane shit... involving shit. She was obsessed with removing it from her body. I think she thought it would make her skinny. I actually told her the only thing it would make her was a colostomy bag wearer when her sphincter stopped working. I said this to her in an airport bathroom when I caught her chugging an entire bottle of Milk of Magnesia – which she would have shipped to herself in various parts of the country or world whenever we had a shoot that involved boarding an airplane. I told her that despite her love of designer logos, Chanel was not making a colostomy bag... yet.

She also liked colonics. A lot. She would get them once a week and would take employees with her to treat them to one as well. This is a fun outing with the boss. Can you say inappropriate? I went three times. The recommended amount of colonics is twice a year. Her colon cleansing place finally banned her from coming. I think they finally realized that the tube shoved up her ass was eventually going to suck out all of her innards and no one in Beverly Hills wants that to happen under their watch.

She liked to hold meetings in the ladies room at the office, where her ass would explode into a bowl and the gaseous farting was louder than anything she was trying to tell us. We would stand around wide-eyed with our mouths and noses covered in disbelief. Someone once very quietly turned to me during an assplosion and said "Oh my God. She's like a donkey." So of course I began calling her that whenever possible in my best Shrek voice. Getting called into the bathroom for a meeting was everyone's worst nightmare, but eventually everyone got shit-nitiated. She would say to you – in the middle of a conversation – "I have to go the bathroom. Come with me," and that would be it. Faces would turn to stone, and you would follow her into that dark abyss, turning back to look at those who knew – they were about to see THE DONKEY.

There were four stalls in this particular work ladies room, and usually by the end of the day at least three stalls would be "blown out," so to speak. She'd knock 'em dead one at a time. You'd walk in to pee, only to fling open that door and find a hot mess of shit and paper clogging up the bowl and the spray reaching to places I didn't think were possible. At least three times a week, the yellow "Caution" stand would come out, and a poor little old Latino man would go in there – like a shit spelunker – looking to find his way down those dark dirty holes. I actually saw her tip him once. Talk about a hostile work environment.

I also once witnessed her take out an entire Winnebago in Cairo during a trip that also exposed her other weight loss method... pissing. She drank a lot of water and took those crazy cancer-causing "star" caps that were pulled off every shelf in every corner of the world. She believed that peeing made you lose weight. She had to piss constantly, and it didn't matter where we were. She forced our driver to pull over in Egypt so that she could pee in what turned out to be a sacred burial ground. Yes, this fifty-something-year-old woman yanked her elastic travel pants down to her ankles and pissed on the side of the road in Cairo and she made another employee stand there and guard her while she did it. It was White Trash Ugly American at its best, and I have never been so horrified.

Some of her employee speeches were also truly inspirational – that is, if you were hoping to be inspired to become The Queen or a dictator. She once told a room full of people, "I have all the money and power, and I don't need any of you to do this job." Unless, of course, she actually wanted the job to get "done," because she sure as hell didn't get her nails dirty. In fact, she got her nails done at the office.

Every morning started with a news meeting and a beauty session in our conference room – which was all glass – forcing everyone to watch the dead skin being pumice-stoned from her feet. (It was bad enough being in these meetings but from the outside it was like watching a really weird TV show.) The blinding stench of nail polish remover wafted through the room and she yelled above the sound of the nail drill as it filed her acrylic nails to perfection. Like characters in a scene from the movie "Marathon Man," we'd all sit around staring and wondering, "Is it safe yet?" She also frequently had her hair colored in this same glass box. It was not unusual to sit through a meeting led by a foiled filled head with dye dripping down her face. Very business-like. In fact, if a man ever did what my female boss did at work and he wasn't a tranny, he'd be fired.

She also delivered her best one on one "pep talks" in that glass box for everyone's viewing pleasure. And by pep talk I mean bitch slap. There's something wonderfully private about being verbally assaulted while the entire staff is watching from their desks. I was fired a total of three times. One of these times, the glass actually rattled. I made the mistake of smiling during this firing, and that was a very bad thing.

The first time I was fired was because I'd put an "ugly picture" of her on the television show we worked for. Her family had called to tell her she looked fat in the shot we used. This became my fault. The real problem was that she had been shoving massive amounts of baguettes down her gullet while pretending to work in Cannes and was actually – fat. She told me to go home and think about what I'd done. I left. She called me 20 minutes later and said, "Isn't this silly? You should come back." I said, "I'm busy now. I made plans for my free afternoon" and hung up.

That was the beginning of the end. After a while, I realized she was actually obsessed with me – and eventually she became the abusive boyfriend I was afraid to break up with. I was working with the enemy, and I was afraid to leave. When I got hair extensions, she got hair extensions. I would dress up for work – she started dressing up for work. Only she couldn't last more than one hour in her outfit, so she would immediately change into her uniform – LuLu Lemon stretch pants, a clingy T-shirt, and some sort of warmup-type jacket. She looked like a bad white rapper – one who refused to wear underpants and a normal bra. She would only wear those paste-ons that went over her nipples – and were clearly visible through her shirts.

The second time I was fired was pretty damn dramatic. She had just had a facelift – her second. She had already had pretty much everything else done to her. In fact, she looked like the meat chart at a butcher shop… or a quilt. This time, however, she had had fat taken from her cheeks and injected into her lips, so she couldn't pronounce any words that began with "p," and the "pl" combo was even more ploblamatic. I picked her up on the side of the road in Beverly Hills. Her face seemed to be smeared with some kind of anti-combustion grease, and she did in fact look as if she might blow up at any given second. She appeared to be high on at least three different medications and was slurring like a drunk. She was very unhappy that I had not supported her with the Big Bosses about a particular promo she had personally written – as a good Number Two was "supposed" to do. It was true – I had not supported her. That was because the promo was also like a Number Two – the kind that comes out of your ass. You know how kidnappers use the expression "proof of life"? Well, this was "proof of crazy," and I was being held hostage and expected to say it was awesome when it was a pile of insane. So I did what no one else in our entire company would do – I told the truth.

I don't even really know how to explain what happened next, but there was convulsing, tears, screaming, and a Beverly Hills door slam exit from my car in the middle of traffic that made "Frankly, Scarlett, I don't give a damn" seem like a pitiful little line. Her last words, screamed through tears, were, "Can you please try and hold it together until I come back from my surgery?" I didn't think I was the one not holding it together. In fact, I wasn't sure if she'd even remember firing me. Sure enough, that night I got a text from her. "The show was great tonight!!!" *Three exclamation points? Wow. It wasn't that great.* Was this her way of saying, "I had a little oopsie in your car, and all is well, and we'll forget it ever happened?" I went back to work the next day, and she continued to email and text random thoughts that seemed as if all <u>was</u> okay.

But about a week later, she returned to work and called me up to some mysterious third-floor conference room we never used. She said these eight little words to me that I would eventually come to fear… "Can I talk to you for a second?" These words would symbolize – "Mommy is mad" – and they were said in the quietest of angry voices. A voice so much louder than her scream. She sat me down to tell me why I was not a good co-executive producer: "You never back me up, and you don't talk to me the way I need to be talked to. I want you to tell me the truth, but I want you to do it in a way that works for me. So when you want to have an opinion that's different than mine or tell me you don't agree with something, just grab my hand and touch it and say 'Baby, baby, we should rethink this.' I want you to talk to me like a wounded baby girl – because that's what I am. I'm a little girl who needs to be talked to in a supportive, gentle way."

I started looking for the cameras, because clearly I was on some new hidden camera show we were developing. Nope. No cameras. So I looked her straight in the eye and said, "I got it." I then went back to my desk and emailed and called every connection I ever had and started looking for a new job.

The last time I was fired was more of a demotion. It happened in London during the Royal Wedding of William and Kate. Now this was a pig fuck of epic proportions. We had taken almost all of our staff to London and were running around like ugly Americans, covering the shit out of this impending marriage. We also had a special correspondent with us. She had an English accent. She also hadn't been popular since about 1982, so I'm not sure what kind of an audience grabber she was, but we paid her $100,000 to smile for the cameras and use as heavy a British accent as she could muster!!!! She was so happy to be standing in front of Buckingham Palace with a camera focused on her that she didn't care what she was saying, so when the Boss Lady asked her to start screaming like a demented child when William and Kate came out for their classic balcony kiss – she turned it up full blast. I was horrified. The famous British wife of a British rock star was also working for us at the time and was the only person not putting up with my boss's shit. She looked right in the face of evil and laughed at her.

The night before the actual Royal Wedding was my last, "Can I talk to you for a second?" moment. I didn't really know why she was mad at me this time. I think it was just a culmination of how shitty an employee she thought I was. I was rude. I was mean. I interrupted her too much. I wasn't in sync with her. I was laughing at someone else's joke. I wasn't laughing at her joke. I was always trying to steal the attention away from her. I never told her what I was doing outside of work. I wasn't her friend. All the other employees were her friends. I needed to share with her. Why couldn't she get close to me anymore? *Blah. Blah. You're so fucking crazy, it's scary.* And then she said something to me I'll never forget – something that finally woke me up from my long national nightmare of a job. She said, "Do you think you're the only person who can write this show? I can replace you tomorrow. You're not that special."

I found Henry and had a full-on breakdown. I was crying and shaking and told him, "That's it. I'm done. Nothing is worth feeling like this – not even Hermes." Well, maybe Hermes, but she never gave me that. I told him I was quitting. He told me to hold on. And then he did the most amazing thing. He put his job on the line and made a call. I listened as he whispered into the phone like a hit man, "We have a problem in London I think you need to know about." He told the person on the other end of that phone the details of what was going on – and when he hung up, we hatched a plan. I would never, ever have to set foot in that office again. He found a way to get me off the Mother Ship – all future anal probes, cancelled. He snuck out of my hotel room like a thief – and for the first time in seven years, I started to breathe.

Moments after he left my room, she walked in, unannounced, no knock. She looked at me and quietly said, "You're a good writer, Heidi." I said, "I know. Now if you don't mind, I have some work to do." She awkwardly turned around and left. I almost threw up. I knew I was about to do something no one else had ever done to her. I was about to tell the truth about what kind of monster she really was. This woman had sucked me in with a lie - pretending to be a normal, supportive friend and boss – and then like every bad boyfriend I had, tried to break me.

I worked through the Royal Wedding and pretended that everything was fine. She told me not to come in to work that Monday, and to think about what I had done and what position I wanted at the company since I clearly could no longer be her Number Two. That day, she emailed and called me incessantly: "Hey, wanna go get pancakes?" she yipped into my voicemail. *Uh, no thanks, I'm a little busy bad-mouthing you all over town.* I never returned a call, an email, or a text. After seven years on the job, I simply never went back. I didn't pack up my office. I didn't say goodbye. I just erased it from my life like a bad dream. Many people have contacted me since I left. They heard we had a giant blowup in London and that I threw a plate at her head. I wish. She tells people that I was mean to her and yelled at her in front of others. I did. I yelled, "Leave me the fuck alone, you crazy bitch." (But I really only did it in my head.)

I am well aware of the expression, "If you don't have anything nice to say, don't say anything at all," but remaining silent won't stop a bully. I think this will. There, I feel better now.

Chapter Three

The Mental Patient

I have a psychic. There, I said it. Let the judging begin. It's an innocent enough thing to say the word "psychic," but when combined with the word "my" to form the phrase "my psychic" – innocence switches to insanity, and you are suddenly Koo-Koo for Cocoa Puffs in the eyes of others. Never ever say the sentence, "Ohmigod, you should totally call my psychic." Unless you're fine with losing that person from your life or at the very least – finding out how quickly they can run.

While other loons are spending thousands of dollars and tens of years talking to a shrink, I spend my money on a little woman named Letty, who may or may not kill things in order to make my dreams come true. If a chicken has to die in order for me to get the job of a lifetime or the man of my future, then so be it. Letty is the most powerful little person I have ever met and I don't mean midget. If she were that, I'd say it because a midget psychic would be the best thing that ever happened to me and I would brag about it.

I first met Letty at the suggestion of a friend who goes to see her at least once a month. The good thing about Letty is – she only charges $37 a visit. I'm not sure how she came up with this random number, or why it's hundreds of dollars less than any other psychic, but I wasn't going to look a gift tarot reader in the mouth. I made my first appointment to go see her. Letty lives somewhere in the Valley in a neighborhood that I'm not even sure has a name. The only landmarks are the dozens of carnecerias that line the streets and the slightly scary-looking residents. I was nervous at first, but I figured Letty would know better than to live in a dangerous neighborhood, right? I mean, she's psychic, people.

She directed me to sit at her kitchen table, and quietly started to lay down some Tarot cards while I sat there babbling like a loon. "So nice to meet you! I've heard so much about you! This is so exciting!" *Blah. Blah. Shut up, Heidi .You sound insane.*

And then she stopped. She took a deep breath. She turned to me and slowly asked, "Why are you so sad?" I burst into tears. It was a complete cry explosion, the kind where your shoulders shake and you sob so hard the snot is pouring out of you. It was a cry that was many years in the making, and it scared the hell out of me. I had just left the worst job in the world and was terrified that the boss I'd ratted out to human resources was going to come after me. I was sad. I was destroyed, actually. I had no idea what I was going to do next, and I was quickly running out of money. It was the reason I'd come to see Letty in the first place, but I didn't let her know that –I wanted her to guess. That's what we untrusting Jews do. We test people – even psychic people.

After the sobbing subsided, Letty said, "There's a woman who is going to say some terrible things about you." *Bingo!* "This woman is in love with you. Is she a lesbian? She's very jealous of you." Letty didn't even wait for me to respond. She just kept spewing. "I don't know what you did, but I know you are confused about it, and I'm here to tell you, you did the right thing. This woman is not good. She only cares about power and money. She will soon have neither." *Yay! Yay! Yay! "How much will it cost me to destroy her?" I wondered.* Thirty-seven dollars seemed too low a price to crush someone's soul. But Letty informed me that I had nothing to do with the downfall of this woman's life – it was her karma that was going to get her. Darn it. I so wanted to help.

Letty told me *I* was going to be fine and that I'd never have to worry about money. (Clearly, she's never seen my Barney's credit card bill.) She gave me a bunch of candles to light when I got home and said that I would be working on a scripted television show, which at the time was completely ridiculous, but of course is now completely true. She told me that I should stop thinking so much, be grateful for the things I already had, and just open my doors to letting things happen. Now granted, Peaches, my French Mastiff, would have been dead-on if she'd told me the same things, but there's something about Letty that makes you believe. She told me quite a few things that first session. They were all right on the nose, and when I left I was truly smiling from ear to ear. I was a new woman. Some Dr. Lie-On-My-Couch-While-I-Pretend-To-Listen would never have charged $37.

I've continued to see Letty for various reasons. The best thing she ever did for me was to stop my crazy neighbor from harassing me. This awful woman who lives on my block once kicked Peaches in the face because she thought Peaches was running up to her to bite her and not just to say "hello." She kicked Peaches, so Peaches bit her - as she should have – and as I would have if someone had kicked me in the face. I wanted to kick her in the face but instead I drove her to the hospital. I paid for her time there. I delivered food to her house and picked up anything she needed for about two weeks. I felt badly even though it was her fault. For over a year after that, she emailed me and called me on an almost daily basis, telling me that she should have my vicious dog put down. I wanted to have *her* put down. This should be an option in life for bad people. Instead, I found a picture of her online and took it to Letty. My little card reader made a huge "X" over the woman's mouth, taped the picture to a candle, and placed that candle on her mantle. Apparently, Letty's mantle is very special. It's her altar. And I think we all know what happens when Santorians put stuff on their altars. Shit happens. Bad shit. That woman has never spoken to me again. It's been three years. I have wanted to use this Letty hex on about 200 other people, but I haven't done it – yet. I'm keeping a list. So stay in line.

Psychics may be a load of crap who tell us what we want to hear, but they've helped me to find some kind of inner peace. When a total stranger tells me something that I already know, I find it comforting. And when Letty tells me she's put all my bad thoughts and people trying to hurt me in a coconut, and that I should throw it and break it to kill the demons – I'm gonna throw that coconut. Hopefully the next time I won't throw it so close to my car, though. It knocked off my side view mirror–and that cost way more than $37.

Psychics aren't the only people I throw good money at. I also enjoy a Trance Channeler. This is someone who goes into a trance and literally channels a dead person to talk through them. Back in the 80's, I went to a Trance Channeler in New York City. The name of the dead spirit

I spoke to was Tomo. He was an Indian. He mapped out my future 25 years ago, and every single thing he said has come true. No joke. I remember very clearly the day I went to see Tomo who when I walked into the apartment, was a woman, named Cathy. She sat in a chair across from me, turned on a tape recorder, and went into a trance. She told me that while she was under her trance, Tomo would ask me a few questions. I was freaking out.

Cathy went into her trance and then suddenly – Tomo started talking. He spoke very slowly. He asked me my name and then took a giant pause. Cathy later told me it was like he was looking up names in a big book and then reading what was written about that person. "You are very big for someone so small," he said. "I see you at your desk in your glasses, and you are in California, and you are writing. Millions of people will hear the words you write." *Okay, well this is dumb. I have perfect vision, and I'm not a writer.* (I am now, folks. Nail, meet head.)

Tomo went on to tell me all kinds of things without my saying one single word. He would ask me for a name of someone I was curious about – just the name – and then he would pause and speak. I asked him about one complete psychopath I had dated. Tomo told me this person looked like the Oscar statue – all beautiful on the outside, but hard and impenetrable. He was in fact a model—a model asshole who once pointed a gun at my head.

And then came the real reason I had gone to see Tomo. I was heartbroken. I had fallen in love with someone who was about to get married. I didn't know this when I met him. He decided to keep that a secret. We met through work and would hang out all the time. We'd go to lunch almost every day, but nothing ever happened.

I wondered why he never tried to kiss me or do anything, and then one day when he dropped me off at my house, he finally kissed me lightly on the lips, and I fainted. My knees buckled under me right there on 14th Street. The whole thing was very intense. The next day, we went for lunch, and when I brought up what had happened, he said, "Well, it's hard because I'm getting married, you know?" *Umm, yeah. No, I didn't know, you complete dickhead.* I got up from the table and said, "Please don't ever call me or contact me again." And I walked away. Crushed.

I had an incredible connection with this man, and I was having an extremely difficult time getting over him. I would sit in my apartment and sob. I needed a quick fix. I told Tomo the guy's name. He paused. And then he said, "The reason this relationship cannot be completed in this life is because it was completed in another. You know this man. He was either your husband or your brother." *Oooooo, creepy.* Tomo said he could see us in our past life like a movie. He said we were in a boat, and I was wearing a big yellow hat, and I was laughing and laughing, and I was so happy. He said that I would one day meet the man of my dreams, and together we would be like a beautiful dance. I have never forgotten those words. I have yet to meet my beautiful dance.

I left feeling better. Maybe this was a bunch of hogwash, but I didn't care because I had finally stopped crying. Many months later, the man who'd broken my heart called me. He was now married. He said he thought about me all the time. He said he had just watched a movie called "Cousins." "I think you should watch it. It reminded me so much of us, but I'm not sure why," he told me. I ran out immediately and rented that movie. It was not a great movie, and I kept sitting there thinking, "*What the hell is it about this movie that's like us?*" It was about cousins who fall in love, but couldn't really get together because they're related. I mean, we weren't related, but we were sort of kept apart by strange circumstances – those circumstances being he was a giant liar who hid his fiancée. Then came the last scene of the movie. Ted Danson and Isabella Rossellini on a boat . Uh-oh. Isabella is wearing a giant yellow hat. Double uh-oh. The final shot was a close-up of Isabella on a boat in her big yellow hat – laughing and laughing and laughing. And scene. Fade to black. It was nuts. I was suddenly cured. The end. Stick a fork in that guy. Over and out.

Years later, I went to see another psychic. I was struggling in my career a bit and was considering a change. I was trying to write a romantic comedy about a woman who realized her life was about to end because she had cervical cancer and she hadn't yet met her soul mate. (Funny, no?) The psychic said I should make the cancer – breast cancer. I went home and finished the movie, and indeed made it about breast cancer. Sometime later, that married man contacted me once again. He said he had been thinking about me. I asked him how his wife was. He said, "She died of breast cancer last year." And scene. Again.

Over the years, many different tarot card readers have laid out many different versions of my life and how they think things will unfold, but other than Tomo and his beautiful dance, they all seem to share one common thought when it comes to men – they don't see any. Zero. None. Empty. Sorry. They all get to that love life part in the reading, lay out a few cards – and then silence. They look up at me sheepishly and then change the subject really fast. I'd love to know what it is they're seeing, but I'm afraid to ask. It looks really bad. There's usually that devil card, and a sword, and something with blood dripping off of it.

Letty recently told me that there were dozens of men just waiting for me – but that I had to let my walls down. My walls are down. And so are my pants. Let's go, people.

Chapter Four

The Dating Game

I had an abortion on Yom Kippur. This pretty much sums up the success level of my dating life. I decided to kill a baby on the highest of Jewish holidays because I hated the semen provider so much I had to have whatever he had deposited in me removed immediately before I sat down with my parents for a slice of challah and some nice brisket. Anyone who tells you getting an abortion is easy is a big fat liar. Sure, physically it's fairly simple. Emotionally, it's a shit storm. I pretended it didn't destroy me, but it did. I still think about it today. That child would be 26 years old now, which means – I could date him.

What I know about dating you could fit on the head of an extra-small pin, but I have learned one thing that I believe is the key to success for all relationships: If you want a man to fall in love with you, tell him to go fuck himself. He'll never stop calling. Men want what they can't have. If you can keep up the lie that you're not really that interested in him throughout the beginning of your relationship, then congratulations – you have no soul, but you will have a husband. Later in life, you'll have to start acting interested, or he'll leave you for a 25-year-old who thinks he's fascinating because he has a job with an assistant and his own couch. But in the beginning: Act like a bitch, and he'll crawl over glass to get you and lock you down.

I once overheard a young lady say to her date, "I think I could fall in love with you." The translation of this statement is, "I am not only madly in love with you already; I am seconds away from having a full-on nervous breakdown if you don't say you're in love with me too. I am, in fact, obsessed with you. I've already memorized your social security number and your license plate, and as soon as I get a raise, I'm having you tailed by a private detective. I broke into your Facebook account and secretly follow you on Twitter under an assumed name." This statement is so thick in psychosis, it should be considered the line that makes you excuse yourself to go to the bathroom and hightail it out of whatever situation you're in. This goes for men and women. If you say this out loud to someone, don't get upset if they run.

I've only had a handful of actual relationships in all of my years. I'm not good at them. Or they're not good at me. I was way better at one-night stands. I had a lot of those. I do remember all of the relationships I did have – and how they ended. They have shaped me in some way. Good or bad. But mostly I'm gonna have to go with bad, because eventually they are what stopped me from bothering with this nonsense. The stages in a breakup are the exact same stages there are to grief. They just differ slightly based on who's doing the breaking. Denial. Anger. Bargaining. Depression. Acceptance.

When someone breaks up with you, the stages go something like this:

Denial-Please don't leave me. I'll change.
Anger-You are an asshole for dumping me.

Bargaining – I will take that statement back if you take me back.

Depression – I am going to kill myself or at the very least – eat this tub of chocolate icing.

Acceptance – I accept that I am amazing, you are an asshole, and I need to lose 10 pounds.

When you break up with someone, the stages go something like this:

Denial – No really, I'll call you later. (You never call)

Anger – God, why won't he stop calling me?

Bargaining – If you convince him to stop calling me, I will pay you.

Depression – God, why did he stop calling me?

Acceptance – Maybe I should call him.

Basically, when it comes to dating – If I like you, I like you, and I don't have time for games. I also don't have time to immerse myself in your life. I'm a pretty independent woman. I don't need you to hold my purse while I shop, and I don't need to go to the gym with you. I can occupy my day all on my own-some, thank you very much. I have found the word "independent" is catnip to some men. They smell it from a mile away and need to bat it around before they completely destroy it. This has been my dating experience over and over again. I like to call it "The Bait and Switch." Here's how it works: You – the very together, very cool girl – meet a seemingly very together, very cool guy. He says, "You're the most independent person I've ever met." He then spends months trying to destroy that independent person, so that she is no longer able to make rational decisions like, "Wow, I should stop dating this abusive asshole."

This is how I got on a train to Abortionville on Yom Kippur. I was dating a model. He was beautiful. He was a cocaine addict. And he was all mine. Yay me! I met him at the China Club in New York. I couldn't believe a hot model wanted to date me. I was so overwhelmed by his beauty that I ignored all the signs that said – get out now. The day I found out I was pregnant, he screamed at me for an hour, telling me that it was my fault. I went to the abortion clinic on my own. I thank God I had the right to make that choice. No one needed a tiny version of that shithead walking around. I let him move in with me, and I worked two jobs to support his cocaine habit, while he never went to work and slept with countless other women behind my back and one time – right in front of my face.

After the abortion, he went to a friend's wedding that I couldn't attend. A few weeks later, she asked me to edit her wedding video for her. It was your typical video – bride kisses groom, bride eats cake, groom does toast, boyfriend makes out with girl on dance floor – wait, what? Yes, my boyfriend was caught on tape making out with some wedding guest. Gotcha! Tears. Vomiting. Sadness. Etc. I lost my shit. I went home and changed the locks immediately. I packed up all of his belongings and piled them in front of our apartment door. I left a note: "Go live with the chick in the video." I heard him outside the door for what felt like hours. He was probably trying to teach himself to read. I still Google his name on a monthly basis. I'm hoping there's an article that says he's dead. I never find anything. If I do find out he's alive, I'm going to be very busy, hunting him down and killing him.

Not so shockingly, there have been bigger douchebags on my dating dance card. I remember the night I lost my virginity. It is one of my life experiences that is, unfortunately, seared into my brain. I was in college and had just turned 18. I had waited because I thought it was the right thing to do, and I wanted to give this very special gift of my unbroken vagina to the right person. When the right person didn't come along, I got really drunk and gave it to the hottest guy I could find. I think his name was Steve. It was one of the most traumatic experiences of my life. I sort of forgot to tell him that I was a virgin, and when he saw blood all over his sheets, he thought he had killed me. I thought this would be the beginning of a beautifully fucked-up relationship, but Steve quickly ignored me after he deflowered me. The only time he spoke to me again was across the room at our local bar. He held up a cherry between his two fingers and crushed it. Then he laughed maniacally, like a Disney movie villain. Steve later got into a very bad accident while driving drunk and was severely brain damaged. Karma is a bitch.

The only time it's sort of difficult not having a boyfriend is around the holidays. And that's only because of the looks you get from coupled people. That, "You poor thing, you're so alone, what a loser" look. The worst of these holidays is, of course, February 14th.

Holidays that are related to people being in love make me want to go on a killing spree. I mean, it's taken me years, but I finally know why Cupid carries a sack of arrows. It's not to shoot unsuspecting victims and make them fall in love with each other – because that's a childish and stupid concept – and it's what horrible dating websites are for. No, Cupid's arrows are a defense weapon against people like me, who want to drop his fat little naked ass out of the air and stop the bullshit.

I know it's not unique to hate Valentine's Day. In fact, it's rather clichéd. And you know what? I'm fine with that. Call me clichéd. Tell me I'm bitter because someone hasn't handed me a box of chocolate since the days when I didn't care about calories. (For those keeping count, it was about age 11.) It's not my fault that my hopes and dreams are pinned on a red satin, heart-shaped box. It's Hallmark's... or Oliver's – the four-year-old boy I loved before I knew what love was.

When I was a little girl back in the 1800's, going to school on Valentine's Day was thrilling. This was the day you would find out which boy liked you, and if you were lucky, there would be more than one. In the classroom, there would be a box in the back where you would secretly put your card for your valentine, and then the teacher would hand them out. I loved these little cards, and even at the age of six or eight I loved getting more than one. Greedy little bitch. Boys would also give you boxes of chocolate their mothers had bought, or candy bracelets, and all would be right with the world because a fellow seven-year-old had proclaimed his love for you with a heart filled with cancer-causing deliciousness.

I didn't do anything unusual for the candy, like show my underpants behind the activity center or let someone play doctor with me in the nap area – I was just a nice little girl. Life was so simple back then. Someone liked you – they gave you a secret card. Now I realize that I was set up for failure on February 14th all those years ago, and it's been a giant disappointment ever since. Now I realize that knowing if I'm loved is directly tied to this day in February. Valentine's Day made me feel special and important and pretty. All these years later, it hasn't changed. I want a big heart-shaped box filled with deliciously crappy chocolates, and the bigger the box, the better. I don't care if the chocolates come from RiteAid or Ralph's supermarket or some weird dude on the street with a cart. I just want to remember the joy of the days when Valentine's Day was a holiday I loved and looked forward to. Hallmark has been making me feel like a big, fat, alone loser, and I want to sue them for years of torment.

These days if you want to meet a boy – you need a computer. A lot of my girlfriends have met their boyfriends through one of those dating websites. They have no problem going on hundreds of dates to find their prince. This to me is like accepting a job where all you do is get interviewed by awful men over and over again. "What's your favorite movie? What do you like to do when you're not working?" For the record, the answers are: "Diner or Field of Dreams" and "Eat stuff in bed." I have a white Jewish girlfriend who only dates black men. If you look up "Jew" in the dictionary, she's there waving a brisket while bathing in that 1970's soda – TAB. She has nothing in common with black men – except Common – whom she once banged. I dated a black man once. I was not cool enough to pull this off.

I decided to sign up for one of those dating websites – let's call it Z Gallery dot com – because it felt like furniture shopping. I'll take a gray couch with hard cushions that looks modern, but is really vintage. They should have called it Saggy Nads dot com, because after browsing the pictures from my so called "match" list, I was pretty sure no one's balls had been anywhere near their penises for years. I mean, don't get me wrong, my shit has moved, but these guys were old – really old. After giving it a full 15 minutes, I decided this was not the way for me to meet someone. I was catapulted into a depression from these photos, and I thought if I don't get off this website now, someone will find out I'm on it – and I will be labeled a loser for the rest of my life.

After a while, I totally forgot that I had even signed up for online dating. Then came the exciting news in my inbox. "You have 24 new matches!" I couldn't help myself. I started scanning the pictures, and once again it became crystal-clear to me that the only place my matches had been for dinner was jail. There was a guy named "Popeye" who was dentally challenged. There was "LonelyMa," who had either forgotten the "n," or was in fact looking for a mother. There was William, pictured in full military gear complete with gun. And these were the top choices. There was no way I was going to go out into the world and meet one of these people somewhere for dinner or drinks. In fact, the only place I would ever go to meet them is a police station. Every single one of my "matches" looked like he'd make soup out of me and my bones, which he'd pick clean after I said something annoying, like "Can we go to a movie tonight?" I really don't understand how people make a connection on a computer and then physically go meet that person and think this is a good, safe idea. I was vetted for this website about as well as my dog was. In fact, I once signed Peaches up – and she got 45 dates in one day.

I think my main problem with the whole dating thing is – most of my so-called relationships took place while I was highly intoxicated, and nothing good can come from something that starts with the words, "Sorry I puked on you" or "Yes, that is my pee on your sheets, but it was an accident because I dreamed I was peeing and then I did." The older I got, the more confident I got – and the less I dated. I don't know what the mathematical equation is, but I think it's "Me equals single squared."

I may be done with dating, but apparently my vagina isn't. I send myself emails all day with little things that make me think, or make me curious, or just something that strikes me as funny. I have to write them down because I forget them 10 seconds after I think of them. I love going through the notes at the end of the day, and sometimes I don't even remember thinking the thought I had, but eventually everything comes back to me. Except for this note, which appeared in my inbox three times: "To do list: Go on a date." I don't remember writing it. This leads me to one conclusion – my vagina now has a laptop or an iPhone and is sending me emails about what it would like to do – over and over again. It seems my vagina and I have lost touch and are now living completely separate lives. I do feel badly for it, but I'm not really sure what to do.

Maybe I should get my vagina a listing on match.com, but then the question becomes, how do I fill out its questionnaire? I have no idea what kind of music it likes or its favorite kind of takeout food. I don't know if it likes tall or short penises, dark or blonde. I've never bothered to ask. The truth of the matter is, when you're not shoving your lady parts up against some male bits – there really is no reason to pay attention to your vagina.

And if you're not touching it – you can lose touch with it – and so it seems, my vagina and I are having some kind of a communication breakdown. In fact, my vagina might actually be broken. Maybe I should write a letter to Santa and ask for a new one. I assume the fat man is the one who handles stuff like that. Jews don't have anyone to write to and ask for stuff. We should get someone.

The bottom line is "Vagina – I'm just not that into you." I feel like every time I pay too much attention to it – it just gets super needy and has to be involved in every decision I make. Do we have to do everything together? Sometimes I just want to be alone. I'm thinking maybe we should watch You Porn together – God knows everyone tells me that's what I'm supposed to be using my iPad for - but again, I don't even know what kind of porn it's into. Schoolgirl? Cheerleader? Girl on girl? Boy on boy? Boy on girl? Dog with cat? I probably should stop calling it "it," but I'm not one of those women who's going to name my vagina. In fact, if you're a girl who calls her vagina something other than "Vagina," you're an idiot.

But I decided that if my vagina really wanted to go on a date – I should get it prepared, and so I took it to get waxed. *When do I get to stop doing this? At what point will I look down and say, "Ah, fuck it?"* I know there are a lot of women out there who don't put themselves through the torture of having hot wax poured on them by a total stranger, and granted, my waxer has been more intimate with my clitoris than most men I know, but I feel like I need to keep shit tight down there – at least for now. I will say the concept of lying down on the table with my knees in my nose at the age of 80 is not cool with me – at all. I mean, when I'm an octogenarian, will I have my knees pinned behind my ears while someone waxes my ass crack? What will we talk about, my waxer and I? It's already an awkward conversation. "So what do you do for a living? Did you want the lips done too?" I don't know if a bald vagina is a good look on a granny, but when your choices are gray hair or no hair – all roads point to the full muff.

If I do start dating again, I'm also going to have to overhaul my underwear system because as of now – I'm having a full on Granny Panty love affair. I bought a six-pack yesterday at CVS that cost about $12. They are cut below the butt cheeks and come up to my waist, and I don't think a pair of underpants has ever made me happier. I feel free. I feel like dancing. I feel like wearing them out with a pair of high heels and my new fake eyelashes and singing, "Here I am, world." They aren't riding up my ass and cutting into my hips. They also can't be worn under any item of clothing. I might as well wrap myself in a Hefty bag and try to shove that inside my skinny jeans.

My gynecologist once told me that g-string underwear is basically a fecal delivery system to your vagina. And barf. Isn't that sexy? I don't wear those any more. I only wear boy-cut briefs. They still ride up your ass. I can't tell you the amount of times I've been caught with my hand shoved up my crack pulling something lacy out of my nether regions. It happens every time I do it. I think – "*I really shouldn't pull these out right now*" – but then the pain gets to be too much and so I try to gingerly reach behind and nip at the panties. But inevitably, I do a really fast clean-and-jerk, and then I turn around and voila – whoever the cutest guy in the room is, he's staring at me and my crack-retrieval moment. I'm sure it would be easier to just not wear underpants, but I don't understand this concept at all. Girls who wear short skirts without underwear are only asking for one thing – me to see their vaginas. I don't want to see your vagina. I don't even want to see mine.

I believe the world of women is separated into two groups– those who wear undies and those who don't, and I don't want to know anyone who doesn't wear them – especially the ones who talk about it constantly. I don't want to sit on a chair or a couch or a car seat that your vagina just sat on. It can't possibly be sanitary. I don't know where your vagina has been and if you don't wear underwear, I bet you don't either. I love wearing boy's boxer brief underpants. They are so comfortable, though you need a big bush to fill out the penis area. Why can't someone invent a pair of panties that are pretty and lacy and don't end up shoved inside my anal cavity to the point where I need a special tool to retrieve them? I don't think that's asking for too much.

The hardest part about being single is how many people are willing to point it out to you – like you don't already know you're a societal loser. They say, "Why aren't you dating someone? You're awesome," as if it must be my fault that I'm single, and I know what the reason is, and I'm doing nothing about it because I'm an asshole. The truth of the matter is, married people just want all the single people hooked up so that they aren't the only ones who are miserable. I love the people in a hideous marriage who give you dating advice about a second after they tell you their husband makes them want to vomit inside their own mouths. They'll say, "You really need to open yourself up to love. You're so close-minded." *Yes, you are correct, because look how well it's turned out for you being married to a mouth-breather with more hair on his back than my French Mastiffs.*

There's even a commercial that proves how horrendous marriage is. I'm sure you've seen it and simply didn't realize the real message that was hiding underneath. The ad features a woman sitting across the dinner table from her husband. Her voice-over says the following: "You know the little song he'll hum as he gets dressed. You know the shirt he'll choose. The wine he'll order. You know him. Yet now, after exploring vineyards in the hills of Italy, he doesn't order the wine he always orders. He asks to be surprised. And for that moment. He's new to you. Princess Cruises. Come back new."

Now, let me tell you what she was really saying:

"You know the little song he'll hum as he gets dressed."
YOU'VE ASKED HIM TO STOP A THOUSAND TIMES, AND THE NEXT TIME HE DOES IT, YOU WILL STAB HIM IN THE EYE WITH A FORK. YOU HATE THAT SONG. IT MAKES YOU MENTAL.

"You know the shirt he'll choose."
YOU'VE TRIED TO THROW THE SHIRT OUT TEN BILLION TIMES. IT HAS A SPAGHETTI STAIN ON THE FRONT AND PIT STAINS UNDER THE ARMS. YOU HATE THAT SHIRT ALMOST AS MUCH AS YOU HATE HIM.

"The wine he'll order."
HE HAS NEVER ASKED ONCE IF YOU'D LIKE TO CHOOSE THE WINE. HE DOESN'T CARE IF YOU LIKE IT OR NOT. SHUT UP.

"You know him."
YOU HATE HIM.

"Yet now, after exploring vineyards in the hills of Italy."

WHICH YOU HAD TO TRY TO TALK HIM INTO FOR 10 YEARS. HE NEVER WANTS TO GO ANYWHERE. HE WHINED THE WHOLE TIME.

"He doesn't order the wine he always orders."

HE STILL DIDN'T ASK YOU. HE JUST DECIDED TO WING IT.

"He asks to be surprised."

HE'S TOO BORED AND OLD TO CHOOSE. HE'S FINALLY BEEN WORN DOWN. THANK YOU, JESUS.

"And for that moment -he's new to you."

HUH, MAYBE YOU'RE NOT SO HIDEOUS AFTER ALL.

"Princess Cruises. Come back new."

FUNNY... I KINDA DO FEEL LIKE A CRUISE. BY MYSELF. THANKS, PRINCESS.

It's not that I dislike men – I actually think they're quite fantastic – I just don't want to go hunt one down. I'm not a hunter... I'm a gatherer. So if there's a store I can go to and gather up a few to test out – I'm in.

Even my dreams about dating are screwy. Just the other night – this went down in my sleep. I was in some sort of office or waiting room while two young men and their parents completed applications to go on a date with me. They were both in their twenties, and I was not really attracted to either one of them. I didn't want to tell the parents of one of the kids he was most definitely gay, but it didn't matter because the cuter one filled his application out quicker and that's how he won... me. So, there we were on our way to dinner downtown (in downtown Manhattan, I believe) with his parents, when we ran into my friend Dan. Dan didn't think we should go all the way downtown. He thought we should go where he was going, right around the corner from where we were. This sounded great to me – the less time with this whole situation, the better. Once we got to the restaurant, I went to the bathroom and immediately became overwhelmed with how bad my hair looked. This kid wasn't so hideous after all, and I really needed to pull myself together. I couldn't find the right lipstick, and I was in there for so long that the waitress actually had to come get me so that the other people at my table could order already.

When I came out of the bathroom, the Mom and Dad were gone – replaced by a table full of this guy's friends and one of my old co-workers, Diana M., whom I hadn't seen in ages. Before I could say, "Thank God you're here" and talk to her, she left, and in came my friend Chelsea K. with her agent and a very small dog. She was freaked out because some paparazzi had leaked her address, and now she was being stalked. We discussed the fact that she should move and probably go get her Mom, whom she had left in the house – alone. I finally sat down with my date (can't remember his name) and his weird young friends, and I kept not getting the chance to talk to him and I thought he was avoiding me, so now I really liked him a lot and thought he was really cute.

Finally the dream dissolved to some outside area, where I was now in a beach chair next to the Dream Boat. I could now tell he liked me after all, as he started telling me he didn't like women his age (clearly the dream part). Suddenly we were back at the table and an older woman – whom I thought was his friend – showed up. It turned out to be his mother – a different one from earlier – and it turned out she knew me from when I worked at Extra. She said, "Aren't you like fifty someth…" Suddenly, my date piped in and said "Forty-two. She's 42." Uh-oh. I didn't remember lying to him, but it seemed I had, and it seemed the jig was up. This woman was totally going to take me down.

Then my sister Wendy called and asked me to come meet her for drinks at her apartment. Apparently, she lived in a high-rise in Manhattan and I lived on the floor below her. Suddenly, I was driving in my car and my date was running alongside my car window, wanting to come with me. All I could think was, *"My bedroom's a mess, and I don't remember if I'm waxed or not. Crap, this is happening!!"* So off we went in my car, but the highway was pitch black, and we got totally lost and almost died in a crash. We couldn't see any signs. Somehow we ended up at his house, and he decided to change. He had two lookalike brothers who lived with him, and when I went to go use the bathroom, his mother walked in on me and yelled at me for dating her much-too-young son. But she couldn't stop us. I picked up my Chanel purse, which was sopping wet because his cat had peed on it, and off we went.

I finally got my navigation system to work, but we decided to stop at a store first and get some snacks. A homeless man stuck his tongue on our car window and started fucking with my windshield wiper. Suddenly, my date's sister was sitting in the car with us as my date got out to deal with the man. We started screaming, "No! Don't mess with him," but before we knew it, the homeless guy had stabbed my date in the neck. My date didn't seem to think it was a big deal, but there was blood everywhere. I called the paramedics, and the only thing I could think was... *"Well, looks like this date is over."* And that's when I woke up.

In conclusion, I believe, the moral of this story is... Don't waste your money on Chanel, because some cat will just pee on it and if you date me, you will die.

The other thing I totally forgot to do was have children. People who have them love to remind me that I've missed out on the single greatest opportunity there is in life. People with children sometimes say the darnedest things to single childless people... and by darnedest, I mean – dumb, stupid, inane, insulting, ridiculous, and for a big finish let me whip out my favorite word... retarded. Go ahead and report me to the National Association of Retards. I don't care. I love the word "retard." I had to give up "that's so gay" and "you're so queer," so I'm keeping "retard." You can all go fuck yourselves.

Recently a woman I work with returned from maternity leave, and after we all oohed and ahhhed over pictures of her miracle child – sorry, but I find my dogs more interesting – someone said something so awful that I instantly wished a plague on all of their houses: "Now you know what real love is, right?" My head snapped so quickly, I'm still stunned it didn't spin right off my spine and roll into the community kitchen. "Oh," I said. "So, I'll never know what real love is? Wow, thanks for that." I laughed it off. Hahahahaha. "I'll have you know that tonight when I get home, I'm going to make out with Tulip, whom I love." The person said, "Oh is that your dog?" "Yes," I said. And we laughed and laughed and laughed and I thought, *"How quickly can I stab the person who said that and run out of here without anyone seeing me?"*

Now, I am unclear why I am living this life single and childless. Maybe it's my choice. Maybe it's not. I don't spend a lot of my day wondering about it. I am too busy living my life and loving it. Really loving it. Why did I forget to have kids? I don't know. But I haven't heard that many convincing stories that I'm missing something so spectacular. You married people and parental people may love what you're doing, but you certainly don't act that way. Forget gay-bashing – I'm single-bashed on a daily basis and I'm not gonna lie, I'm exhausted by it. If someone's not reminding me that I don't know what real love is because I don't have children, they're reminding me I'm single by saying things like, "But you're so pretty. Why don't you have a boyfriend?" First of all, I had no idea that if you're considered pretty, you get a boyfriend. Sorry, ugly people. And second of all, what am I missing that you people want me hooked up so badly--other than the sex, which quite frankly, it sounds like none of you are having?

I know that some of my friends just want to see me in a relationship because they believe that I will be happier and that my bitchiness is due to the fact that I'm single. It's not. Also, if one more person says, "You need to get laid" after I say something mean to them, I will have sex with them and prove to them that I'm still mean when its done. Sex is not the gateway to kindness. Your penis is not the hug I need at the end of the day. I don't need your penis. I need you to stop doing shit that makes me act like a bitch. Here's the deal: I am not against boyfriends. I just don't have one. I am not against children. I just don't have any. These things are all subject to change. Except the kids part, because my eggs are too old, and "retard" may be my favorite word, but I don't think it would be right to knowingly give birth to one.

I mean, I love myself so much it hurts, but I really never felt the need to create a carbon copy of me. I guess I could always adopt a kid so I have someone to burden later in life. I do worry about who's going to change my diaper when I'm drooling all over the canasta table at my Retirement Village, but I have some time to figure that one out.

Chapter Five

Welcome to Florida, Here's Your Noodle

I haven't seen mine yet, but apparently all Jews have a contract with God or Jesus or somebody really important that says when you hit 65, you must move to Florida. I have no idea how Florida became the Hebrew Beltway, but it is. Maybe the heat is similar to Israel – but I've never been to the Holy Land. I don't want to die in a grocery store. People tell me every day how beautiful Israel is and how I'm an idiot for not going but I'm sorry – I'm not jumping out of an airplane and I'm not going to a country that is in a constant state of war, where crazy people strap bombs to themselves as routinely as I wipe my ass.

What I do know about moving to Florida is that once you get there, time stands still. How else can I explain that my parents still don't have "call waiting," and I constantly get a busy signal when I call them? Who are they talking to anyway? They are so busy. My parents have a bigger social calendar than I do. It seems like there is a lot to do at their over 55 Floridian Complex in Delray Beach. I'm pretty excited for when I move there.

I lost about six hours of my life one day trying to get my parents on Facebook. I could have taught them how to build a rocket ship quicker. If you want to know the true meaning of guilt, yell at your parents. It's akin to screaming at a three legged puppy. I know we didn't choose our parents, but seriously, how can you ever get angry at the people who gave you the gift of life? Now, I am as hard and cynical as they get, but I am so grateful just to be breathing. I don't know if the alternative is cloud dancing and cocktails, so I really truly do relish being here on the ground among the living.

I think my parents are here to remind me to be nice to old people. Oh, and to tell me gossip about the kids I grew up with. According to them, I am the only successful one. The other kids are massive fucktards and can't keep a job or a woman or a house or a calendar. I hate to be the bearer of bad news to my parents, but I have no kids, no husband, the bank owns my house and quite frankly, my career could end tomorrow. But fiddle dee dee, why let them worry about reality? I have also come to realize that my parents are here to inform me of all deaths of people I don't remember. The conversation goes something like this:

Mom: "Remember Bobby Feldersomethingwitz?"
Me: "No."
Mom: "He was married to Jodie Blahblahstein?"
Me: "Sort of."
Mom: "Well, he's dead."
Me: "Okay. Thanks?"

My parents are British. My dad is from Leeds, England and my mother from Liverpool. If you think this makes them cool and hip and Beatle-like parents – you are wrong. They are still Jews after all, and that trumps "cool" every time. My parents moved to America when they first got married back in the '50s, and for some reason they thought it was a brilliant idea to move from England to Staten Island. This would later prove to be a horrible decision – unless you enjoy living on a landfill surrounded by Mafia – but I'm sure it seemed like a wonderful idea at the time. I hate telling people I was born in Staten Island and in fact, I tell people I was born in France. I believe that the Statue of Liberty – a gift from France that you can see from Staten Island – is our own little Isle de la Cite. It works for me.

The problem with having British parents is that the English are about as different from New Yorkers as you can get. They don't emote the same way and in fact, they don't really emote at all. The British are refined and reserved and keep their feelings in check. This does not fly in America, and this is a really hard way to grow up in a city where all people do is to shout their emotions and stab you in the front with their feelings. The good thing about having British parents is their complete lack of knowledge of American children. I got away with murder as a kid. I started drinking at age 13 – and was smoking pot at about the same age. I dropped mescaline to go to school and tried pretty much every drug before I ever got to college. I even got high with my history teacher. My parents had zero idea. They just thought I sucked at school because I was stupid, which I may very well have been. (Have you ever met a smart 13-year-old?)

Everyone loved my parents. They dressed well and threw fabulous cocktail parties. But they were big believers in "Children should be seen and not heard," and sitting around the dinner table in our house was SILENT. There was no shouting or arguing allowed. You would enjoy your Veal Cordon Bleu in silence, and you would eat everything on your plate even if it took until 2 am. I don't understand this concept at all. If my child wanted to only eat one pea at dinner I'd be fine with that. She'd be thin.

My house was also very, very neat, and there were a few rooms we weren't even allowed in unless we were serving guests at a dinner party or performing for them. I once played a song I wrote on the guitar for a bunch of my parents' party guests. It was about a hooker. My mother was not pleased. When we were very small, our parents took us into the dining room to teach us manners. We spent the whole meal saying, "Please pass the salt" and learning to use our knives and forks correctly. I am super- grateful for this, actually. I find the way some people eat akin to watching monkeys throw their own poo at the zoo.

If you'd walked into my childhood bedroom, you would have thought I had just moved in that morning. We were not allowed to hang pictures or have any kind of mess. All I wanted to do was hang posters of Bobby Sherman and David Cassidy, but that was not allowed. It would ruin the paint. I shared a room with my sister Alison, who lived in the upper part of the room that was separated from mine by one step. If I ever stepped on her "part," I would be beaten to a pulp. All the dressers and closets were on my "part," so she had full access. This was how I learned the concept of "unfair." I was the baby. Everything in my life was unfair. Everything was monitored, even our phone conversations. We had one of those little telephone tables that sat in the hallway between the two upstairs bedrooms, and that's where you had to have your conversations with your friends. When no one was paying attention, I would try to drag that phone into my room. You could JUST get it inside behind the door and barely shut it – but it was better than being out in the open. You kids with your cell phones today have no idea how hard it was to be attached to a land line—a rotary phone land line. Our phone number started with "Gibraltar 8." That's how old I am. I might as well have been making calls from my covered wagon.

I was not allowed out of the house at all during the week until I went to college, and the first night there I went completely mental and partied like an animal. It has taken me 30 years to reign myself back in. My parents told me nothing about sex. In fact, they told me nothing about everything. I freaked out the first time I got my period. I had no idea what it was. I figured my vagina had died. My mother shoved a tampon at me like I was an idiot. *How could I not know these things?* This was not the conversation a refined British woman was supposed to be having with some sweaty 13-year-old. Even if that 13-year-old was her kid. I most definitely did not grow up in some real-life version of "Sex and The City." Back in the '70s, girls didn't talk about that kind of stuff. No one was walking around Susan Wagner High School shouting, "Hey, you bleeding yet?" I miss the '70s.

I went to visit my parents recently after I was reminded that it had been a while since I'd been to Florida – about 10 years. The idea of spending time in my parents' condo was not exactly number one on my "to-do" list. It was, however, number one on my "to-don't" list. I booked my ticket and emailed my flight info to my Dad. He wrote back: "Can't wait to see you. Even if only for a day." *What? A day?* I looked at my itinerary and yes, I had in fact booked a trip for just 24 hours. Oops. I told my folks it was an oversight and rebooked my flight. I figured I'd go for three days, but I don't know how to tell time and thought that a flight that leaves at 12:05 pm on Wednesday meant that you leave

Wednesday night and not five minutes after midnight on Tuesday. Now I was going to Florida for four whole days, and what the hell was I going to do for four whole days? *Ohmigod, I should rebook this but then they'll get upset! Breathe.* I broke out in hives.

"I'm so happy you're here!" my mother cried as she hugged me moments after I landed in Florida. "I made you a home-cooked meal tonight in honor of your trip. Brisket and chicken soup!" I then informed my mother that I had been a vegan for the past four months and hadn't had meat in about a year. Her face fell. I ate the brisket. It was going to be a long four days.

Delray Beach is like a giant summer camp for old people. My Mom and Dad's complex had everything I had back at Camp Indian Head. There was a pool and a clubhouse, and there was a constant variety of things for them to do. My first day there, we stopped at the clubhouse and I met a bunch of ladies playing bridge, Mahjong, and even canasta. I thought all of these games died years ago, and now I'm worried that I'm running out of time to learn them and won't be allowed in some of these communities when it's my time to check in because I am Mahjong-illiterate.

The second you start meeting your parents' friends, you find out what your parents really think about you and lucky for me, my parents seemed to think I was pretty great. In fact, some of the people I was meeting thought I was probably too great to be true and when they met me they kind of rolled their eyes at how much they had been forced to hear about me: "Your mother can't stop talking about you and that show you write. What's it called again?" I thought, *"I know you know what it's called, you smug old people."*

Every day we would go to the pool, because that's where the action is in a Florida condo development. I could have sat at that pool and listened to people all day long, which is a good thing because old people know how to talk. All the women would gather in the pool with their noodles. If you don't know what these are, they are long Styrofoam things that help you float. Apparently when you check in to my parents' community, they give you a noodle. (I hope I get to choose my color. I want pink.) I met a woman named Pearl who I instantly fell in love with. She floated out to the pool area like Jackie O. She has short white cropped hair and wore big black round sunglasses. She had on a one-shoulder navy blue swimsuit and was pin thin. I get the feeling people tell Pearl she's too skinny and should eat more. To me – she was perfection. She was beyond chic. Pearl walked up to me and said, "I've heard so much about you, and I just want you to know that I appreciate celebrities and your mother doesn't. You should have been my child. I want to hear everything you know about the stars. I should have been a star. Either that or a princess." I couldn't agree more. I thought – *"I want to be Pearl when I grow up."* Pearl's husband Hank takes her to the pool each day to make sure she gets her exercise. It seems Pearl can be a bit petulant when it comes to doing things she doesn't want to do. This made me love her more.

On my second day in Delray, I met "Mr. Turkey Timer." This was the nickname I gave to the man who came to the pool every day and began a ritual that I instantly knew had been years in the making. The pool area at my parents' place is fairly large. There are plenty of places to sit without being on top of anyone else, and yet this minute man would always sit right next to me.

He would arrive in shorts, a T-shirt, and those hideous Velcro mandals men wear that should be outlawed. He would spread two towels out on a chair, one for the top half and one for the bottom. He would apply lotion and then get out the kitchen timer, set it, and lie down. Then for the next 20 minutes, the sound of that dammed timer would drive me insane. TicK. TiCK. TICK. I wanted to scream, "How about a watch? Has this age-old system failed you in some way, sir?" He once spoke the word "hello" to my dad. I detected a slight accent, and my brain decided it was German and then that brain went off on an entire "Timer=Oven=Jews=Death Camp" rant. What can I say – that's how all Jews think. Every time I hear Heidi Klum say anything, the translation in my head is, "Get in the oven. Get in the shower." I can't even step foot in Germany. It's a whole thing. Something must have gone terribly wrong in "Mr. Turkey Timer's" past tanning days that led him to this system. It worked for him. I decided to keep my mouth shut and my headphones on.

One day, I overheard this conversation.

Man: "You know what I'm gonna do today? I'm gonna go out and get myself some of that – what's it called – that smelly stuff – Faberge? Yeah, Faberge. I'm gonna get some of that Faberge. I'm gonna light a Cohiba and I'm gonna pour myself some wodka (he actually said "wodka") and then I'm gonna smoke the cohiba and drink the wodka and then I'm gonna spray the place down so she don't know nothing about anything." (He was referring to Febreeze and how he could have a moment of happiness in his home without his wife finding out.) I thought, *"Eighty-something, and still hiding things from a spouse? Color me permanently single."*

The most amazing thing I saw, however, was while driving down the highway to dinner one night. Suddenly there was an electronic sign for a "Silver Alert." I asked my dad what that meant.

Dad: "Old people missing."

I laughed for a full five minutes. And dinner itself is a whole thing in Florida. The most popular time to go is about 5:30 which is when NO ONE is hungry and the portions you get are the size of your head. No one can eat the size of the meals they give you, and so everyone gets a doggie bag. This makes the diners extremely happy. Basically, if they don't get two meals out of the one meal – the place is shit and they're never going there again.

My parents are now in their 80's, and I have to say, I'm thrilled with their aging progress – it bodes well for me. They both have their minds completely intact. No one is drooling and mumbling things incoherently – at least not without the aid of vodka. The only real problem is loss of hearing. My Dad wears a hearing aid, which does not stop me from having to scream everything. When you say things like I say on a regular basis, screaming anything should not be an option. My Mom's hearing is also on a slippery slope to non- existence, but she refuses to wear a hearing aid. I get it. They're not at all sexy. I'm terrified of losing my hearing. My Mom says you basically just hear the sound of your own voice in your head. Uh-oh. I already have that problem, and it led to some severe drinking. At the beginning of my trip I thought, *"How am I going to survive four days here?"*, and by the end of it, I was thinking, *"I'm so glad I spent this time with my parents"* – well, that and, *"I've got to start a retirement fund immediately."*

I studied Kabbalah for a couple of years. It's some 4,000-year old-mystical side of Judaism, and they believe in reincarnation and that we actually choose our parents. They say that when we are souls in heaven, we decide which people will raise us in our next lives based on things we need to learn. I'm not sure what I needed to learn other than the obvious – Jewish guilt – but I'm so glad I chose my parents. I may not understand why they did what they did when it comes to how they raised me, but I think I turned out okay. When I was young I wished my parents were more like my friends' parents. The girls were all really close with their Moms and did things together and gossiped about boys and clothes and how to frost-tip their hair. But as I've grown, I've realized you can't change people, and you have to just accept them for who they are. So I accept my parents for who they are – the wonderful people who breathed life into me and love me unconditionally. My parents accept me for who I am – the loud-mouthed weirdo who can't seem to find a man and didn't give them grand kids. My Mom may not have spent nights braiding my hair and showing me how to scrapbook and whispering to me all of life's secrets, but before I left Florida she told me she was glad I was leaving my sneakers in the guest closet so she could look at them and think of me when I wasn't there. It broke my heart.

I'm not as scared about getting old since my visit. I may even check in to my parent's complex when I hit 60. I'll be the spring chicken in the group. I even have my eye on one single old geezer who was pretty sexy. I've got my fingers crossed he doesn't bite it before I get there. Together we'll swim with our noodles and he'll think I'm the sexiest young thing in Del Ray Beach. Finally, I'll be able to start eating again. I can almost taste the cake now.

Chapter Six

I'm Starving

The nicest thing you can ever say to me is, "You look anorexic." Those words should always be followed by a "thank you" and dare I say – a hug. If you're lucky enough to hear this phrase, it will most likely be said to you by a woman. A man will never say this to you, because a man has no concept of "too skinny." All men are looking for sticks with tits. The second a woman says, "You look anorexic," smile and hug her because it means you look perfect. Any woman who tells you that men hate skinny girls is a liar and probably a fatty. Please tell me the last time you saw a hot guy with a girl who doesn't look like she needs to eat a steak. If you're a girl who tells other girls they look anorexic, please press pause before you say it, and realize that at your core, you are truly jealous of how teensy tiny she looks. Realize that her bird-like body is making you angry. I know I will not be happy with my weight until a stranger stops me on the street and says, "We need to get you something to eat immediately. You are way too thin." If someone isn't trying to tie me down and feed me intravenously – I'm too fat.

I feel like I've been dieting since birth. For all I know, I cut off my feeding tube in the womb because I was getting too chunky. I have tried every diet known to man (isn't that expression interesting?), from the cabbage soup one to the baby food one. Baby food is low in calories. Unless you eat all of the jars in all of the land at once. I ate seven jars in one sitting. It's true what they say: Banana is the best. If I had a kid, it would starve to death because Mommy ate all the food.

Usually after about three days on a diet, I just get a new scale because I'm convinced that's what the problem is. The only way you can really tell is by your clothes, which is why I keep all of my Fat Pants. They hang in the closet next to my Skinny Jeans, reminding them that we are all just a hanger away from Chunkerville. It's like one happy dysfunctional family. I bet they talk to each other when I close the door at night, with the Fat Pants mocking the Skinny Jeans for lack of wear and how I have to lie down on my bed '70s-style to zip them up.

It's impossible to know what size you really are anymore because designers are constantly messing with us and lowering the sizes of their clothes. Clearly they all got together and said, "Let's convince people they are skinnier and change the way we label things." The only thing more brilliant than that was the creation of the "boyfriend jean." This is the most ingenious way of selling fat pants I've ever seen. My boyfriend jeans are a size 27, and they're swimming on me, but that's because they're a size 8 Fat Pants. We all know the truth. Just because you give them a cute name doesn't make me thinner. If you can fit into your boyfriend's jeans, you need a diet.

Every day, a new study comes out that tells me what I *have* been eating to lose weight is now the number-one fat builder in the entire universe. One second you're eating cardboard-flavored pasta, and the next you're chowing down on some berries that came out of a koala bear's ass. Women will do anything to lose weight, except give up shoes and purses. I am currently addicted to a diet ice cream cone that has only 150 calories and is most likely made of cancer. The problem is that I eat the entire box in one sitting, which pretty much kills the low-calorie concept. I need a supermarket that only has single servings of everything. I used to do the low-carb thing, but I needed a math degree and an atom-splitter to really figure out just how many carbs were in something. The box lies. I'm just saying.

I have no "off" button when it comes to food. I dream about my prison meal constantly. This is the last meal you get on death row, right before they "off" you. You can have anything you want. There are no limits. I'm not sure why I have a prison meal, because the only thing I might go to prison for is murdering someone who calls me fat, but I do have one – and you should too. I am not ashamed to admit that I judge others by what their prison meal is. My Dad told me his prison meal is soup. Jesus, that's depressing. I mean – they already give you soup. There has to be something more you want. My prison meal changes quite a bit, but it always includes cake. Cake is the most important meal of the day. Anything can be cured with cake. I love the cheapest supermarket kind of cake you can find. I adore the grainy, gritty icing and those giant pink flowers.

I am so food-obsessed that I cannot keep anything good in the house and by "good," I mean anything with any kind of taste. I tend to wake up at 2 am to eat, and I'll eat anything. I once took down jar of Marshmallow Fluff. Don't ask me why I had Marshmallow Fluff in the house in the first place. My refrigerator usually only has condiments in it, and my pantry is filled with things no one needs – like cloth napkins and corn-on-the-cob holders.

I have also eaten out of my garbage can. Pause. Vomit. Rinse. Repeat. It's true. I'm not proud of it, but I've done it – more than once. In fact, I've done it so many times that I now have to take my garbage out of the house and down the street to someone else's cans after a dinner party, because if there are any leftovers in the garbage, they will soon be in my belly. The reason the leftovers have to go in the cans down the street is because I once ate out of my own street garbage can, and my neighbors saw me. I had to pretend I'd thrown out a receipt. I made mini-cheesecakes just last week, and after I ate one, I threw the rest away and then spent the entire rest of the night just opening the cupboard where my garbage can is and eating out of it like it was a cookie jar or in this case – a mini cheesecake delivery system.

I tried putting perfectly good chocolate chip cookies down the garbage disposal once, but that didn't work. I had mistakenly bought the bag the night before and was afraid that if I kept the cookies around one second longer, I would inhale them faster than you can say" fatty fatty two by four." I had made it through an entire morning and afternoon without eating them, but now it was night-time again, and that's when the Sugar Vampire comes out and starts tearing into the cabinets looking to feed. So – I took the four chocolate chip cookies and shoved them into the garbage disposal, turned the water on, and flipped the switch. All of a sudden, the sound of metal being chewed by metal ripped through the house. I turned off the water, then the disposal, took out the cookies, and removed one of those tiny dessert spoons I own, but don't know why, from the unit. Then I shoved the cookies back in, turned on the water, turned on the disposal, and again – metal-shredding, ear-bleeding sounds came from the sink.

I turned the water and the disposal off again, took the cookies out again, and retrieved yet another dessert spoon. Once again, the cookies went back in, the water went back on, the disposal switch was flipped and yes – once again something that sounded remarkably like silverware was being eaten in my disposal. I shut it all down again, pulled the cookies out again, and pulled out a third and final spoon. It was like some kind of magician's disposal. This thing was literally creating dessert spoons down in that deep dark hole. I didn't put the cookies back in right away, because I looked at that disposal and I thought to myself, *"God wants me to eat these cookies. God put those spoons in there to stop the destruction of four perfectly good and, might I add, very sturdy, chocolate chip cookies."* I didn't eat them. But I wanted to.

My girlfriend once emailed me at 2:22 am to ask if it was okay to eat a bag of Nestle chocolate chips. I was able to answer her right away, because I was up eating a bar of baking chocolate. This doesn't even taste good. But that did not stop me. I told her, "Of course it's okay. Isn't that why you buy them?" (I know she's not baking cookies. Jews don't bake cookies. Jews buy cookies.)

I realized that if I could just figure out how to sleep through the night, I would lose 10 pounds instantly. I constantly wake up with food wrappers and crumbs around me in my bed – remnants of a sleepy, fat-filled binge. If I had a boyfriend this activity would never happen. No woman is getting up in the middle of the night and bringing a chocolate cake to bed, and if she is, she should probably get a divorce. But getting a boyfriend just to curb my voracious nighttime appetite seemed a bit extreme. So I got the next best thing – sleeping pills.

Now I have tried every kind of sleeping pill there is, from the prescribed, like Ambien, Lunesta, and yes, even Klonopin, to the natural, like melatonin and some kind of root that tasted like dirt mixed with poo. There were a few things that made me see things while awake – like double rainbows – and a few that made me see things while asleep – like murderous bloody rampages with me as a knife- wielding killer lunatic. I would have taken sleep-eating or sleep-driving, but sleep-killing seemed a bit over the top. I didn't have trouble falling asleep; it was staying asleep that became problematic. *Did I snore? Was that waking me up?* Again, this would be a good time to have an all-male sleepover, but the end game was them discovering I sounded like my grandmother, and that didn't seem fun.

I've thought about tape-recording myself to find out what is waking me up at night. But I already know what that would look like. Me going to sleep. Me waking up. Me getting up to pee. Me going back to sleep. Me waking up. Me watching television on my iPad. Me going back to sleep. Me waking up. Me changing pajamas because mine are soaking wet. Me going back to sleep. Me waking up and going downstairs to eat a block of cheese or make a snack tray to take back to bed. Me going back to sleep with gum in my mouth. Me waking up because I swallowed the gum. Me going back to sleep. Me waking up 10 minutes before the alarm goes off. Fun.

My doctor decided that it wasn't a sleeping problem, but an anxiety problem, and said that I was afraid to sleep in my house and woke up frequently to make sure there were no intruders. First of all, by "doctor," I mean the guy I pay 10 bucks to see because he's in my health plan. Second of all, I have two 120-pound dogs – only an idiot would break into my house because the barking, thrashing, and charging of the doors and windows when they hear a leaf blow by is earth-shattering. However, I like my doctor, so I decided to try something he said would work. It's called Sinequan. I took it for about a year, and for the most part it worked pretty well, but I had also gained some weight at the same time and was having a really hard time losing it. That's when I discovered the horror. I Googled the sleeping pill, and the second I typed in the words "Sinequan and…" the words "WEIGHT GAIN" popped up. And that was the end of that drug. I mean, the words "WEIGHT GAIN" will stop me from doing anything. I could be dating John Hamm, but if I see "WILL CAUSE WEIGHT GAIN" when I Google his name, I'll dump his ass faster than you can say "Modern-Day Fred Flintstone."

I've tried exercising to lose weight, but they say that your body weight is 80 percent what you eat, which means mine is 80 percent cake. I can't seem to find an exercise system that doesn't make me want to die. I've done them all –Yoga, Pilates, Bar Method, Aerobics, Step, etc. I like them for a few months, and then I'm miserable and finding excuses not to go to class, like – I'm tired. I used to go to something called "Barry's Boot Camp." Kim Kardashian was in my class a few times. Her ass is remarkable. It's like a table. I wanted to rest my water on it - and my towel - and my keys, purse, and shoes. There was room.

Recently, I made the huge mistake of looking at myself naked in the mirror, and I noticed that I now have back rings. If you don't know what back rings are, congratulations, you win. They are rolls of fat on your back. They are indentations you should have at your waist, but they sit above that area and fold over. Go look at your Mom – she has them. I don't want them. I was so upset by this discovery that I almost didn't get dessert at dinner, and I almost didn't stop at the grocery store on the way home to buy a bag of peanut butter chocolate chip cookies that I almost didn't eat in bed.

Kate Moss once said, "Nothing tastes as good as skinny feels," but that's a lie, because nothing tasted as good as the cupcake I had for lunch yesterday. People say to me all the time, "Why are you worried about what you're eating, you're so skinny?" *Because I haven't eaten in like a year!!*

If you really want to see what kind of damage a small woman can do with food, watch me eat the week before my period starts. This is the time of the month I literally can't stop shoving things down my cake hole. I am careening through my 50s, and I still get my period. This is not useful to me. I could find more things to do with a chainsaw. I do not need to be fertile. If I have any eggs left, they have most definitely expired and if I could reproduce, I would absolutely pop out a retard. I can't wait until the day I start menopause. I will celebrate by eating a cake. From a supermarket or out of the garbage. Whichever comes first.

Chapter Seven

Press Pause

I woke up the other morning 15 pounds heavier than I was when I went to bed. Like a tick that fed through the night, I had blown up. Big. This is not an unusual feeling for any woman – in fact, we check to see if we're fat before we check to see if we're breathing. But I didn't THINK I was fifteen pounds heavier... I actually WAS. I got on that dreaded scale I hide under the sink and sure enough – 15 pounds – overnight. I moved the scale to another room, because surely the floor was uneven in the bathroom and it was throwing things off. I climbed on again in my bedroom. Fifteen pounds heavier. I took off all my clothes and took out my night guard – it could be heavy, who knows? Back on the scale. Fifteen pounds heavier. I was running out of rooms to stand in and things to take off. I would have cut off a limb if I'd thought it would make the scale read lower. Fifteen pounds on a girl just under 5'4" is equivalent to 100 pounds on a normal-height person. "Ohmigod, what is happening?" I yelled to the two dogs staring at me. "This thing must be broken." First thing on my to-do list, get a new scale.

The other situation was my breasts – they were huge. None of my bras fit. *How did this happen while I was sleeping? Is there an Implant Fairy? Had I unknowingly put my boobs under my pillow and asked him to bring me a new pair?* (And yes, the implant fairy would definitely be a dude.) I know small-breasted women think tits are the greatest thing, but I'm here to tell you they are totally overrated. I'm sure that if a guy went to bed and woke up with a bigger penis, he'd immediately go out without his pants and fling it around, but I was not happy with this situation. I already had big boobs for a small person, and now they were porn star-size. Something had to be done. I mean, you can't live a normal life with giant hooters. Note to all you numbskulls getting implants: Boys think big boobs equals stupid – or sex addict. So if that's what you're going for – get it girl – but that was not what I wanted out of life. I've discovered it's fairly impossible to have an actual conversation about anything other than your boobs with a man when you have a couple of grenades stuffed down your shirt. You can, however, get them to do pretty much anything. Cleavage equals mind control. All male eyes go to the boobs. And from what I can tell – the boobs tell very interesting stories to men – stories they cannot tear themselves away from.

I started researching bra minimizers and found a place in Century City that specializes in putting women in the right bra. Did you know that 85% of all women are wearing the wrong one? That was the sign in the window of Intimacy– home of the expert bra fit expert. I had heard about this type of store before–a magical place where some mammtastic genius uses measuring tape and calculus and figures out how to make your giant balloons look smaller and make you feel 10 pounds thinner. I walked in and met Doreen – The Boob Whisperer. I told Doreen my situation – that I really wanted 34 Bs, but I'm a 36 DD. Doreen laughed in my face. "A DD?" she said. "No you're not. That's ridiculous. We'll get you in a room and get your real size right away. You're way bigger than a DD." Uh-oh.

Doreen was very excited about all the options there were for me. I told her what I really wanted was breast reduction surgery. Doreen looked at me like I'd said, "I want to cook and eat small children because they're high in fiber." She recoiled in horror. She asked, "Why would you want to be butchered like that? You don't need a reduction. You just need the right bra." Doreen sized up my naked chest and said, "I'll be right back. I'm pretty sure you're a G cup." *Whhhhhaaaaaattttttt????*

I think I passed out and clunked my head on a mannequin, because when I came to, I was in a room surrounded by lacy, wiry things that had more hydraulics than a cherry picker. *"These are bras?"* I thought. They looked like hats – for two-headed people. There were bras big enough to hide my Chihuahua – in one cup alone. They were massive. They were tit tanks. We slipped one on and – holy shit, she was right. Instantly my boobs were back where they used to be – on my chest, not by my navel. The straps weren't cutting into my shoulders like razor blades. "See?" Doreen said. "We take all the flesh from the chest and push it into the cups and voila." Five hundred dollars later, I was a new woman—a broke woman, but a smaller-breasted woman.

Unfortunately, days later, the reality truly set in. Moving all that shit up had created a new problem – massive back fat. There was so much stuff shoved up, that new stuff was spilling out and over, not to mention that when I took the new bras off, the weight that fell was almost back-breaking. Suddenly, I stopped hugging people. A hug was a pipeline to my back fat. I wanted to put instructions or hand prints on my back to show where people should place their hands– like those feet they put on the dance floor when you're at the Arthur Murray dance school. *What was happening to me????*

I decided it was time to call in the real expert, Dr. Fred. Freddy has been one of my closest friends for more than 20 years, and it just so happens that he's a genius doctor. Unfortunately, he lives in New York, so I am constantly texting him ridiculous questions about my health issues while he's in the middle of seeing patients, like "I have a spot on my cheek I didn't have yesterday. Am I dying?" Or, "Is there a bone in your ass, and is it possible to break it?" Or, "Can you mix Vicodin with white wine?" He always has an answer, and he never, ever judges me. I bet no one tells their doctor the truth about anything, because you know they're immediately discussing your shit over a cappuccino in the doctors' lounge. Freddy would never do that. So, I texted him my latest query: "How did I gain 15 pounds and six bra sizes overnight?" Waiting. Waiting. Waiting. And boom - there it was – in 14-point Helvetica. "Perimenopause." *I'm sorry, Peri who?* "Perimenopause. And get used to it, because the weight isn't going anywhere anytime soon." I burst into tears – overly emotional moments, another little gift from the prequel to the pause. Fred informed me that I was in fact over 50– and that meant my body was going to go into menopause any day now. But apparently, women don't have to just suffer through one hideous life transition – we need a warm up exercise, a training camp for menopause. Peri-menopause. Have you ever noticed that all the bad things in life for women include the three letters MEN?   MENstruate. MENopause. MEN. It's a sign, people.

Dr. Freddy told me to take something called Estrosense, which already sounded like a bad commercial... "I no longer have an embarrassing extra 15 pounds because I have the Estrosense to take this supplement." I went and got the tablets immediately at one of those health food stores that always smells like someone is dying or already dead in the back by the alfalfa sprouts. The Estrosense smelled like estro-ass, but after a few weeks on the pills, I noticed a miracle in my T-shirts – my boobs actually started shrinking. I made it back to a D cup.

But the boob drama was really just the beginning of my maiden voyage into menopause. All kinds of stuff started happening, especially when it came to my period. There's a really old joke about not trusting anything that bleeds for five days and lives. Well, I'm clocking in at well over three decades, so what does that say about me? Sometimes I look down at my vagina and yell, "DIE ALREADY!!" but it's not listening. I think there should be a law that says if you are over 50 and still get your period, you are allowed to do all things a handicapped person does, and you will be sent a giant red placard with a "P" on it to hang from your car's rear view mirror. Fifty-year-olds with their periods should not have to do anything stressful, like walk too far from the parking lot to the grocery store, and we should most definitely be allowed to drive in the carpool lane.

I can ruin just about every pair of decent underwear and/or pants I own with a spectacular and embarrassing bleed-through. Every woman in the world has regular underwear and "period panties." You wear the stained ones when you forget to do laundry, and you pray no one thinks you're cute that day and wants to have sex with you during your lunch hour because that would expose your stained undies. Bleeding through your outfit is super-annoying. Someone should invent underwear that beeps the second blood hits it. Like how your car beeps when you back up and are about to hit something. How is it possible not to know you're about to over flow? It's like practicing the piano five days a month for more than 30 years and still not being able to play "Chopsticks"!

How could I have been doing something for so long and still suck at it? Shouldn't I know by now when a tampon is "full"? And by the way – who the hell invented that? I suppose it's better than a massive wad of cotton shoved in your underpants that makes you walk funny and look like you have a penis and balls so big you pull them back towards your ass, but that string hanging between my legs should at least play something when pulled. How about a nice tune from that period mix tape Ashton Kutcher made for Natalie Portman in "No Strings Attached"? And let's not even get into how many times I've lost the string.

There is not one woman on earth who has not had her period seep through an outfit at a most inopportune time – like while deep-sea fishing with sharks or on a chair while on a first date. This is why a woman will need very loyal secret service agents when she becomes President. No one needs the Chinese to know you've got a period stain on your desk chair in the Oval Office.

One day while at work in the writer's room, I felt something wet between my legs and actually thought I had peed myself. I'm old and weird stuff is happening all the time, so I thought, *"Maybe I can no longer control the tinkle flow."* But it was my period, and it was massive. It looked like I'd been shot in the vagina. I didn't know what to do. I was in a room full of men who would have simultaneously spew-vomited if they knew I was sitting in a pool of my own menstrual blood. It felt like I had just given birth to a 10-pound blood baby, but I couldn't do the normal thing and shove it into a trash bin like a high school prom girl. I had on dark jeans, so it was hard to tell, but the flow hadn't stopped in my pants. It was all over my chair. The minute I got up everyone would have known. So there I sat, covered in my own embarrassment, and I waited until the end of the day when everyone else had left. People thought it was odd as I was usually the first to flee the area but no, I'm just chillin', thinking about stuff. *See you tomorrow. Bye now. Bye. Buh-bye. See ya. Please go already.*

Finally, when the coast was clear, I wheeled myself on the chair out of the writer's room and into my office and slammed the door shut. Then I scrubbed the shit out of that chair. Then I wrapped a faux fur coat around my waist and drove home – in shame. I can't tell you the number of places I've been out wearing my period pants. It turns out that right before you go into full blown menopause – your vagina has a death scene that rivals a Quentin Tarantino film. My vagina was finally dying, and I couldn't have been happier.

I remember the day it became official. Ironically, my vagina died on Valentine's Day. While most people were wearing red, eating cupcakes, and exchanging cards with their loved ones, I was suddenly feeling thin and not bloated and not in the need of a 15- donut breakfast. Wait a minute – I DIDN'T GET MY PERIOD! Happy Happy Joy Joy – could it be true? I was four days past my usual first day of torment and nothing- nada – no signs of The Curse. Could it be happening? Would this be the month I stopped ruining underpants forever? I have been waiting for this day for decades. I don't need to bleed. I need new shoes. And possibly a neck lift. I decided that I should celebrate this momentous occasion with a party. I figured it's only fair that after years of other peoples' engagements, weddings, and baby births – I should be able to throw a wing-ding and celebrate what matters to me – the ability to wear white whenever the fuck I want. It will be a bon voyage party. I will send out invitations. They will have a picture of a tampon with a circle and cross through it. Everyone will join me in celebrating the death of my vagina. The decorations will be cotton ponies. The goody bags will include white underpants. I will register for gifts somewhere meaningful, like Neiman's shoe department. It will be amazing.

Now if I could just remember things… any things. Turns out menopause fucks with your memory. By the time I get to the end of this sentence, I won't even remember what it is I started writing about. I leave the upstairs of my house with an idea, and by the time I get to the bottom of the steps I have no idea what that idea was and why I now am where I am. I write myself notes and forget to read them. The other day it took me four trips just to get home from the office. First stop – the grocery store. When I got home with groceries, I realized I'd forgotten dog food. I went to the dog food store, and when I got home I realized I'd bought the wrong dog food. I went back to the dog food store and brought home the right food, only to realize I'd forgotten half-and-half from the grocery store, so it was back to the grocery store and then finally home. I'll never get that time back. I could have built a ship.

I'm so paralyzed with fear by what I can't remember that I'm afraid to think about it, because I'll forget to be paralyzed with fear. How is it possible that I know by heart my computer codes, my bank codes, my Facebook log-in, all of my credit card numbers, and the phone numbers of staff members from jobs I no longer work at, but I can't remember to buy cream while I'm standing in the dairy aisle? Clearly I need a Dust Buster to do a once-over in my brain.

And just when I thought weight gain and memory loss were my only two mortal menopause enemies – the hot flashes started. My bed became a swimming pool. I started sweating so much at night that I'd be drenched in the morning, and I don't think I was sleep-running because I'd be thinner if I were jogging at night. Suddenly I was very grateful that the only person in my bed was a dog, because a man might get a little turned off to sleeping with a sweat hog. I actually had to start changing my pajamas halfway through the night. Luckily I'm a pajama hoarder, so I have quite a few pair.

Suddenly, however, the night sweats decided they needed better lighting and started happening during the day, at the worst possible times – like at work in the middle of a meeting. There I was in the conference room writing something on the grease board, and all of a sudden I got extremely hot and sweaty and dizzy. I mean hot like I had just walked into a sauna – white hot – the kind of hot you get right before you barf your brains out. It happened in a flash. (That should have been my first clue.) I went from perfectly fine to "Holy shit, I think I might be dying" in 2.5 seconds.

People started scrambling. "Should we call paramedics? Maybe one of the assistants should take you to a hospital?" The sweat was pouring off of me and my hair was starting to frizz. *"I can't believe this is where*

I'm going to die. And with my hair like this." And then suddenly it hit me. I said, "I think I just had my first hot flash." Several men in the room recoiled in disgust, and I could tell that I'd instantly gone from "that kinda sexy older chick" to "that really old creepy broad whose vagina doesn't work anymore, so don't bother hitting on her." Suddenly I was staring in my own biopic called "Nightmare on Menopause Street." *Terrific.*

Thankfully, the hot flashes didn't last very long, and my body seems to have finally settled into its menopausal state – "The Cellulite State. Home of the Giant Boobs." Sure, I've cried a few times over the babies who will never live in my womb with no view, but at the end of the day there is something to celebrate. If I ever get into a car accident and rushed to the hospital, when they cut off my clothes, the nurses will not be able to say "Uh-oh. Period panties."

Chapter Eight

What a Boob

"What did you do this hiatus?" Jean Luc, the star of the show I write for, asked me after our winter break. "I cut my tits off. You?" He looked at me in horror. "Why would you do that?" he asked. "And more importantly – why didn't you show them to me before you did it?" He was apoplectic. I had spit in the face of God or Mother Nature or whomever it is that hands out boob meat. This is the response most men give you when you tell them you had a breast reduction. They don't get it. It's not in their manual. They would never have a penis reduction. Even if it popped out the bottom of their pants and they hand to tuck it inside their sneakers – getting a penis made smaller is not an option.

The process of becoming a B cup was a long one. It started when I was 10 and finally ended after I turned 50. I hear this is when most women finally decide to give their boob flesh to the highest bidder – aka, the plastic surgeon. That's when we stop caring what you (men) think and take control of the flab sacs that are weighing us down, putting giant indents in our shoulders, and making us tape or safety pin shut all of the openings in all of our button-down shirts.

When I was younger, my breasts were around a C cup, and they were perky. They got me things. And I was okay with that. I used them when I had to. But, over the years, I had grown to be a G cup, as in "gargantuan." When you're barely 5'4" and weigh less than 115 pounds, a G cup looks like you're smuggling two baby heads in your shirt. I was not interested in this look. For the most part, I totally hid my boobs, and whenever I did wear something revealing, I had to spend 10 minutes with whomever had just discovered them, explaining where they'd been…."They're in the boob protection program, and today felt like a safe day."

I think part of the reason I always felt fat is because my boobs made me look like a big girl. That and the fact that I have complete body dysmorphia. One day I went online to price-check a boob reduction, but apparently that's not something plastic surgeons list in this town because the idea of a reduction makes you mentally ill and possibly in need of hospitalization. In fact, just typing the words "reduction" into a computer in California could have gotten me arrested. I love women who have naturally large breasts and aren't afraid to put them out there. You know, women who call their boobs "The Girls." I am not one of those women. I have not named my boobs anything other than "Ick" and "Blech." I wonder if there is some psychological story behind my dislike of large boobs. I doubt I was breast-fed. My grandmother had giant boobs. Maybe being trapped in her house listening to her snore while they rose and fell in the middle of the night is in the back of my mind.

For me – the boob removal thing came down to fashion. I hated the way I looked in clothes. Everything that buttoned in the front had to be taped or sewn shut. I hate the way shirts pull apart over giant boobs. Your tits look like they're trying to "bust" free. If you're not in a porno, this isn't a good look. I'm not a big fan of cleavage. I will never understand why women shove plastic parts into their bodies to get bigger boobs but hey

– to each his (or her) own. For me – it was time for the tits to go. *How hard could this be? It's just a bunch of fat and skin getting cut off, right?* Then I started posing in the mirror, trying to hold my boobs to see how they'd look small. Was I doing the right thing? I called everyone I knew who had had a reduction. They all said the same thing: "You will never be happier." Best thing they'd ever done. I'd had mine for 51 years, and if they were supposed to bring me anything substantial in life, they hadn't – so I thought – well – *let's try on a different size.*

I shared this thought with my friend Victoria– which is weird and kinda insensitive on my part since she'd just had a double mastectomy. But it was her removal of the boobage that made me think – maybe I could do the same thing, but skip the whole cancer part. That seemed uncomfortable. I thought, *"I really want pocket boobs. I want to run on a treadmill and not give myself two black eyes. I want boobs that go unnoticed. I want boobs that stand up without a bra. I want to wear a T-back shirt without some kind of hydraulic contraption underneath. I want dent-free shoulders."* So, I made my appointment.

The plastic surgeon took one look at my breasts and said, "You have great boobs, but they're twice the size they should be for you." I fell in love with her instantly. The heavens opened and angels sang and birds tweeted and Ohmigod, *this is the first person ever who hasn't lied to me about my breasts!!!* I made the decision that day to go under the knife. It took me one more year to finally do it.

On a Thursday in May, in a swanky operating room in Beverly Hills, I became Heidi Clements – Official Member of The Itty Bitty Titty Committee. Yes, I finally had them removed. Three days before the operation, I had to watch a lot of videos about how I could die while having it done. This was not cute. There were also videos that told me what to expect after the operation and how I would have to care for my new baby boobies. These, too, were terrifying. I was told I'd have to have someone take me to my appointment and pick me up when they were done. This was an in-and-out kind of surgery. No hospital stay needed. You take your wrapped-up tits with you and head home. Well, I didn't want anyone to know that I was doing this because I didn't want to listen to a bunch of people tell me I was insane and so I had thought I was going to just drive myself there and then back home. Hahahahahahaha. Moron. I needed someone to stay with me for at least 48 hours, because someone would have to lift things for me, dump my drain sacks, and take care of my two 120-pound dogs.

I decided the most logical thing I could do was to ask – my dog walker – who by the way I barely knew. I would pay her to drive me and pick me up and stay with me and watch the dogs. Genius. *"This way,"* I thought, *"when I act like a crazy bitch, she can't complain because I'm paying her. Plus she doesn't know my friends, so she won't be able to gossip about me."* Again really, Heidi? Now let me tell you, Katie is a saint. She is the sweetest, kindest, coolest person on the planet. But again – I didn't even know how old she was or where she lived. *Oh well, fiddle dee dee. She can drive.*

So on D-Day, we piled into my car – and Katie and I got to know each other for the 40-minute ride to Beverly Hills. We talked about my job, and I showed her a picture of the twin baby girls we work with on the TV show that I write for. She said, "Oh right, twins, they always use twins, right? I know they used twins for the movie they made about my family." I said, "I'm sorry, what? The movie they made about your family?" She said, "Yeah, my family and I were kidnapped." AND STOP THE CAR. Katie told me the story of how her parents bought a motel in Oregon, and on the very first night they opened for business, two seriously messed-up dudes kidnapped them for three days and did some seriously awful shit to her Mom. The whole story was a Lifetime Movie Network movie – which I have actually seen – three times. Sometimes you just never know the things you'll find out while driving to Beverly Hills to have your tits removed.

The doctor's office had told me to stop eating and drinking at midnight the night before my surgery. The operation wasn't until 2pm and I thought to myself, *"This is going to be the toughest part."* I was wrong. The second I walked into the changing room to meet my nurse and put on my surgical clothing, I burst into tears. *Oh, shit. I was gonna go get knocked out and cut up. What the fuck was I thinking? This is my biggest moron move yet! What if the anesthesia didn't work and I felt everything but wasn't able to tell them? I hear that happens. I saw that once on the Heath Channel or the Science Fiction Network. What if I woke up dead? Who would take care of Peaches, Tulip, and Lola? Who would get my shoes?* I was freaking out. Then I had to go lie down in my paper underwear and paper booties and get an IV. Ow. And just when I was starting to calm down, the girl who was in surgery before me came out – screaming and crying bloody murder. It was not good. This was not helping. Apparently she had some issues with drugs that she hadn't disclosed beforehand. My inner voice was screaming, *"Shut that bitch up, or I'm leaving."*

And that's when the angel appeared. The anesthesiologist, or as I like to call him, my future husband. Anyone who can help me sleep the way I did for three hours is husband material. He knocked that crazy bitch right back into slumber land and gave me some drugs to calm me down. She started snoring like Tony Soprano. I told him not to tell me if I snored like that. I didn't want to ruin the princess image that he might have in his head. The doctor came in to mark my breasts. She said, "You have giant boobs. I get why you're doing this. I get why people would tell you that you're crazy." I told her again that I just wanted to be a B cup—a small, unassuming, pretty little B. The doctor said, "They're 600 cc's. I'm gonna take them down to 300 if I can."

I woke up a few hours later in a sports bra. I had no idea what my new boobs looked like underneath that bra, and I didn't look for many days. The doctor told me they wouldn't be "done" for about six weeks. What she meant to say was six months. The first time I finally dared to take a peak at them, I almost passed out. It looked like I had been hit by a bus. They were swollen and misshapen and stitched and yellow and blue and *holy shit, what the hell have I done?* Then I slapped my sports bra back on and tried on a button-down shirt. Again, the heavens opened and the angels sang and the birds tweeted and *ohmigod I don't have to tape my shirt shut because I have perky little boobs.*

I didn't tell my Mom and Dad until it was all over because I knew they would worry too much. When I finally told my Mom she laughed and said. "It's always something with you, Heidi." And she's right. It *is* always something with me. When she finally saw me, she said, "You know what, you were right. You look better. You are very brave." I agree. It was brave. It was also just a teensy bit crazy. But then again, so am I.

About six months after I whacked off that 300 cc's of boob meat – I noticed there were a couple of things that I was still not thrilled with. They were a little bigger than I wanted. I truly would have been happy if they had just left my nipples. And speaking of nipples – mine now looked bigger on my smaller boobs. Not the circular part, but the actual nipples, which before surgery had looked like Ticonderoga pencil eraser tops and now looked like four erasers had been melted together and popped back on my breast. I can poke your eye out from 50 feet away. We'll get to that in a minute.

But my surgeon agreed. She wanted to go back in and "nip-tuck" a couple of things. Turns out my skin had stretched – duh, I'm old – and she wanted to cut off some excess. I was thrilled. Which was odd. But I was. The good news was that I didn't have to get knocked out. It would be local anesthesia. A simple surgery. So I scheduled it for 2:30 pm on a Tuesday afternoon. At 1:30 they called me and said, "Where are you? We called you yesterday and said to show up at 1pm." Well, I don't know who they called, but I'll bet that person was confused. So, I jumped in my car – flew over the canyon and headed for the surgeon's office. My phone rang again. "You didn't eat, did you?" "Umm, yes I did, because I'm having local." Huh, this was starting to sound bad. Then my surgeon called. She'd apparently changed her mind and wanted to knock me out. Could we reschedule? I whined. I really wanted this over with today. She said, "Okay, I guess we can still go local, but it won't be fun."

Fun? Was it supposed to be fun? What part of slicing flesh while awake is fun? Shit – now I was freaking out. *Maybe this is a sign?* When I arrived, my surgeon was standing outside waiting for me. Crap. She was nervous that the local shots would hurt. I thought, *"Should I be registering all of this in the logical part of my brain and come back some other time?"* But that kind of smartness has never been my friend, and so I forged ahead. She shot up my right boob. I didn't feel a thing. We were good to go. I headed for the O.R. and put my smock on. I was ready for my paper underpants but was told I could leave my lower half clothed. So I climbed on the table in skin-tight jeans and leopard boots. All was going well – we were laughing. Telling stories. She was burning and cutting away flesh. No problem. She even told me my burning flesh smelled better than most people's. Not something you put on your resume, but I was proud.

Unfortunately, my mood changed when I made the terrible, horrible mistake of looking up into the light, which reflected what was directly underneath – my boob, looking like a bloody sack of raw meat. I wanted to look away, but I couldn't. It was a horror movie starring my tits. It was a whole new level of gross. But, an hour later, it was all over. I had been awake through all of it – and I have to say – it was kinda cool. I felt like I'd gotten to be a part of something super secret that you don't normally get to see. I drove myself home and even went back to work that afternoon. As for my nipples – she said she could actually snip the tip – so we may be going back for the Tit Trilogy. Stay tuned.

A few days later I had to go in for a checkup – which was good – because I was starting to think my right nipple had become detached. At least it felt that way. Other than that, I had no pain. Well, other than the shooting one under my left armpit. Oh, and the one in my right collar bone. Oh, and the one from the bra that feels like it's stabbing me in the rib. Oh, and the one that felt like my lungs had been removed. Other than that – nothing. Totally good. Oh, and the sleeping part was weird. Other than that – I was fine. Really. But I was also really nauseous. I was headed to my doctor's office to get a bandage changed and suddenly about 20 minutes from my home I thought, *"I'm not going to make it."* I quickly pulled into one of the many strip malls in Los Angeles – the kind with a Starbucks, a Subway, and a Greek something or other that has a name that sounds like a vaginal discharge – and looked for a place to barf. Nothing. I started digging in my back seat and found a Bed, Bath and Beyond bag that had some items I'd intended to return. I dumped the contents and barfed my brains out into it. I guess that's the "Beyond" part.

Suddenly, I felt someone's presence next to me. I looked up from my bag, only to see the most handsome person I know, an actor who guest stars on the show I write for, looking right at me and waving. People wince when they meet him. He's that pretty. (His name is Peter Porte. Stop reading right now and Google him. Your heart will explode. I'll wait.) I quickly wiped my mouth on my sleeve and climbed out of my car to say "hi." He went in for a hug and I told him I'd rather not – as I'd just barfed into the bag I was now holding. He eyed it grotesquely and then looked down to where there was something wet on the ground. He quickly jumped back.

"Oh, that's not my vomit," I said. "It must be someone else's." I wanted to die.

About 10 months after I had my funbags removed, I was ready for the ultimate challenge – bikini shopping. I was heading to a family vacation in Turks and Caicos and was super-stoked about buying a bathing suit that was all the same size, top and bottom – small all around. That is, until I had this conversation with a male friend.

Me: "I can't have cake today. I have to get into a bikini in two weeks."

Him: "A bikini? Why?"

Me: "Well, I'm going on a vacation."

Him: "But why a bikini? How about a nice one-piece?"

Me: "Are you saying what I think you're saying?

Him: "At a certain age, women need to stop wearing bikinis. You should get something with a skirt."

Me: "I bet you didn't think tonight was the night you would die."

Now, I am aware that there are certain items in my closet that I should no longer wear–items that are reserved for much younger women, like tutus and knee socks. There are days where I certainly push the boundaries on these items and wear them anyway, but this whole bikini thing is too much. *I mean – I just got bikini boobs, and now I'm too old to wear a bikini?* I knew I was currently way out of shape, but was I suddenly one of those women who was going to upset other people on the beach? Would strangers point at me and say things the way I point and say things about them, like,"Whoa, does that woman own a mirror? She needs to find a one- piece." In the end, I chose to ignore this man and proudly put the B cup in a bikini. I took a picture of myself and emailed it to him. He probably had no idea who it was in the photo, since I made my sister take it from about 100 feet away. You can't see cellulite from a distance.

A few weeks after my trip, I noticed something very strange happening beneath my new teeny tiny bras – more tit. "I think my boobs are made of memory foam," I said to the poor man joining me for dinner. "It's like I keep cutting them off and they keep growing back. They're the Tempur-Pedic of tits." I took a handful of each one and shook them in his face. "Look at them, don't they look huge?" I asked him. He stared at me. It was a look that said, "Please stop – you're insane." Sure, grabbing your boobs in a restaurant isn't the most convenient place for this type of inquiry, but this is Los Angeles – people do way weirder stuff at dinner. For days, I had become increasingly terrified that my boobs were in fact growing back. I asked all of my reduction buddies, who immediately said, "Oh yeah, mine grew back." *What? This isn't in the breast brochure! I paid good money to have these things lopped off – twice - and that's the way I want them to stay.* I could suddenly feel them – touching the sides of my arms, moving when I ran, and popping out of my very expensive, Cosa Bella bras. What the fuck was happening? I hadn't gained weight. I hadn't been doing anything different. I was stumped. All week I would ask anyone I came into contact with. "What do you think? Do they look bigger to you?" Each time the person confirmed what they've always known about me. I'm nuts. So I tried to ignore it. I called my doctor and scheduled an appointment. I decided I would cut these things down to the nipple if that's what it took. I started wearing my big shirts again. Oh, the humanity. I don't know how most people feel about God and creation, but I'm here to tell you that God is a dude, and he made boobs able to regenerate. What a genius!

Then I woke up one morning, knowing that the first thing I had to do was get my finances in order to go in for a third boob job. Why did I hate these things so much? I don't know. I just did. They annoyed me. But before I got a chance to log on and find out how much money I didn't have, I went to pee – and voila – the answer to all my boob problems. I had my period. So I took a moment to send a memo to my vagina. "You died eight months ago. Please stop. Thank you." At least my tits can rest easy knowing they're safe… for now.

Having plastic surgery is not unusual in LA. In fact, the second you leave the house looking halfway decent, someone will say to you, "Your face looks great! What have you had done?" I have had people say this to me, and I'm never sure how to react since I don't really know if they believe it's an insult or a compliment. I believe it's an insult, because to me it means that I resemble that puppet Madame who is clearly the template for all plastic surgeons in Hollywood. Well it's either Madame or Jack Nicholson as the joker. These must be the two pictures they hand you when you graduate from plastic surgery school.

There's no such thing as "good" plastic surgery – despite how many times the person with the shitty lift tells you her doctor was very "conservative." When you can't move your face and your neck still looks like a chicken, it's not good plastic surgery. People are constantly messing up their faces in this town and convincing themselves they look youthful. I have never heard of a young-looking Platypus. And there isn't anything you can't have nipped or tucked or sucked. While shopping downtown the other day, I eyed a fabulous $7 shirt clearly made from old cat, but when I shared with my friend Gail that I thought this would show the two dreaded fats – both bra and back – she replied, "Oh, I know a guy who can get rid of back fat while you're awake." This is something all Jews have – a guy – for everything that ails you and anything you need done. I dare you to ask a Jew a question about something and not have them say, "I have a guy for that."

Gail decided she wanted to have her eyes done. This is something she doesn't need to do. She's a beautiful woman. She's already had pretty much everything else tightened, including her vagina – a procedure she described to me in detail while I tried to hold back the vomit. I don't want to hear about your youthful labia. In fact, you can keep all vaginal lip discussions on the inside of your head using your quiet voice. But Gail is up for any plastic surgery. She believes it is her birthright. She would have her anal cavity tightened if that surgery were available. The eye surgery was going to cost her $4,000. She made a down payment – apparently her eye surgery was on layaway. Once her eyes were done, everything would fall into place. She'd have the perfect boyfriend and perfect job, and she'd feel perfect when she looked in the mirror. Of course, Gail knows this isn't true, but it's her way of feeling better about herself, and I would never condemn someone for wanting to feel this way. I have been known to the grab the back of my neck to see how it would look if I had those giblets removed, but for me it's easier to just pretend I'm sitting shiva on a regular basis and keep all the mirrors in my house covered. Who needs a mirror when everyone else is so quick to tell you how you look?

So with Gail's eye surgery fast approaching, there was nothing holding her back until... ruh roh... her aging pooch had cataracts. Now he needed eye surgery, and his was going to be even more expensive than hers. Gail could only afford to get one surgery done. This is what you call a Jewish dilemma. It is a problem so steeped in guilt that it becomes paralyzing to make a decision, so Gail did what I had done previously for a vexing problem – she called in the Doggie Psychic to find out if her pooch really "wanted" the surgery. No, I am not lying. In came the psychic. On came the trance. Out came the question. And the answer was, "No, Mommy. I don't want cataract surgery." Clearly, the animal psychic was connected to the Plastic Surgeons Society of Beverly Hills.

I think it's fine to fix your outside, but I think it's harder to fix your inside, and quite frankly, I know a few people who could use that kind of surgery. Just because you've had your face permanently frozen into a smile doesn't make you a happy person. But I did go under the knife, my operation did make me feel more confident, and at the end of the day I'm thrilled that my cups no longer runneth over.

Chapter Nine

Last Call – High Anxiety

If you lived in New York City between the years 1985 and 1996, congratulations – you've seen my tits. Yes, that's right. I used to get drunk in bars and flash anyone who wanted to see them, which in case you're wondering was pretty much anyone. I was a dirty rotten drunken little whore. You can roll your eyes in disgust at me all you want, but I don't care – because I had a good fucking time, literally. That is, until June 20, 2000. **Dateline-Los Angeles: Heidi Clements Quits Drinking.** The head runner in the Moronathon hangs up her shot shoes for good. People around the globe sighed the day I quit drinking – because I was an awesome drunk. I was such a good drunk that I made you look less drunk when you were out with me. This is the kind of liquored-up lady everyone wants to be with.

I drank back when it was okay to drive drunk. I never got a D.U.I, but I did have to walk the line once when I was completely shitfaced, and I passed with flying colors. *Love you L.A.P.D! You rock!!* My friend got pulled over one night while we were drinking wine and barreling through the Hamptons. She went to jail. I invited the cop back to the house for drinks. Our entire beach house went to her arraignment the next morning. We brought coffee and donuts. It was our idea of a cool brunch thing to do.

Once I moved to California, I took the drinking to a whole new level. My favorite liquor store was The Pink

Elephant. Let the irony wash over you. One night I had a girlfriend in from New York, and I took her to my favorite whoring spot in Los Feliz. I picked up a guy and left her at the bar by herself. Aren't I an awesome friend? "Welcome to L.A? See ya!" It's amazing how important you think men are when you're drunk. Hours later, I woke up to the sound of someone banging on my gate. I ran out naked with this dude in tow – now sporting an oven mitt on his penis – to welcome my dear friend back to my apartment. She was thrilled. We stood there in the entranceway for 10 minutes while I tried to whisper-slur to her, "Ask him his name," because I had no idea.

Before I quit drinking, there were a lot of men in a lot of places – including Princess Diana's front lawn at Kensington Palace before she died. Some English idiot I couldn't pick out of a lineup convinced me to hop right over the fence and do it right there. The British were, in fact... coming. I had so many one-night stands fueled by such massive amounts of alcohol that I couldn't even begin to give you a number of how many men I've had sex with. I can, however, give you a number of how many men I've banged since I *quit* drinking 14 years ago – but I won't. He knows who he is.

My vagina is like Katrina – after the hurricane. They say you shouldn't have sex with someone until a year after sobriety. I didn't listen. I banged a big fat liar. Sober sex is the most terrifying experience I've ever had. It scared me single. Having someone insert their flesh stick into my lady parts without a drink is like a scene from "Paranormal Activity." Maybe if I videotape it, I'll see what's going on more clearly, but to tell you the truth, I don't want to see that thing coming at me without a cocktail. *Huh, maybe that's why it's called that?*

There are a million drunken stories I've tried to erase from my head over the years. I was thrown off an airplane once, although I have no memory of this. All I know is that I went to the airport one night to get on an airplane to New York and woke up in my bed in Los Angeles the next morning with my friend on the phone wondering what had happened to me. Man, I would love to see the TSA tape on that one-woman performance. I bet I was wonderful. I'll never know. I still break out in a sweat when I pull up to an American Airlines counter. I'm convinced there's a big bloated picture of me with a circle and slash through it back there with the luggage tags. *"She's here, people. Get security."*

Another one of my crowning drunk achievements was the night I woke up to the police banging on my door with my friend Joey standing behind them. "What the fuck are you doing here?" I yelled through the gate. "We just wanted to make sure you're okay Ma'am." "Why wouldn't I be okay?" I asked. "Well, your friend said he left you outside the Staples Center while he went to get the car and you disappeared." I was at the Staples Center? Wow. Now you'd think this would have been enough to make me stop drinking, but I am no quitter, folks!!! I went on to live out a few more calamities, like hitting another car and running, and meeting my friends at the airport covered in blood because I had cut my wrist open in the back of the limo I'd gone to pick them up in. Still – no quitting for me. *Blah. Blah. Staying hammered, thank you very much.* It's hard to forget some of my greatest drinking tales because I'm still friends with a lot of my drinking buddies from back then, and they love to whip out a great story about what a colossal screw up I was. *Thanks. Really. Shut it down.*

The day I finally did quit drinking was the day I woke up to go to work at 5 am and decided to stay home and drink instead. This seemed like a super-good idea. And that was literally the wake up call. I'm not Oprah. I don't have "Aha!" moments. I have "Oh, shit!" moments. And this was a big one. This was the first time alcohol had prevented me from going to work, and work was all I had. So I did what I thought was the mature thing to do. I continued to get hammered all weekend long, and I called everyone I knew and loved and said "I'm an alcoholic, and I need to quit drinking." I already had a good buzz on and I figured saying the words out loud while drunk would make them easier to say. It didn't necessarily make my message sound that believable. If you slur while telling people you're quitting drinking it may be a little hard for them to swallow. Yet, some people were thrilled with my news. My parents seemed a little perturbed. But even through my chardonnay haze, I knew, if I had to be accountable to people – it would keep me sober.

I did go to two AA meetings, but I found it to be a little too "God Squad" for me – and the idea of turning my troubles over to a higher power worried me. I mean, if God had time to handle my chardonnay problem, then we all have a problem. The first meeting was filled with people who were very angry that no one understood that they had serious life issues and should be excused from any bad behavior while trying to get sober. To me, that's a load of crap. Everyone has issues. We all have to deal with problems on a daily basis, and being an alcoholic doesn't give you an excuse to act like an asshole. What it gives you is memory loss. *"Oh did I call your kid ugly and vomit on your lawn? Sorry, I'm an alcoholic and I was having a bad day."* The only way to fix your bad behavior or face a life problem - is to deal with it – head on. At the second AA meeting I went to, some guy with liquor on his breath hit on me. I never went back. Plus he wasn't cute, and I no longer had the ability to drink someone pretty.

The first six months of sobriety was brutal. I hated everyone. Especially people who could handle their liquor – yeah, those assholes. I still went to bars because I thought this would prove I was a tough mother-fucker. All it did was prove that drunk people are super annoying. Eventually, I stopped thinking about drinking and replaced that addictive behavior with something more acceptable – shoe shopping. Turns out, money can buy happiness – and I know all the stores where they sell it.

One day, I went to see the movie "Flight" with my friend Brian. I had no idea what it was about – other than a pilot, a plane, and maybe some liquor. Two hours later, I was sobbing uncontrollably in the back row of the Arclight Theater Hollywood, and Brian was re-thinking the whole "Hey, wouldn't it be fun to go see a movie" thing. "Flight" is about an alcoholic. A raging, crazy, fall down, can't remember anything... drunk. It's about a person who's willing to ignore all the signs that his life is falling apart in exchange for a drink. Someone I used to be.

Apparently, everyone knew this was what the movie was about – everyone other than me... and Brian. I was caught so off guard by emotions that I just collapsed in a heap. My shoulders were shuddering. The tears started pouring out of my eyes. My emotion was shocking even to me. Brian was frozen with fear. Fear that I was broken. We sat there until I was able to calm down a bit. We both realized that I had some shit I had clearly never dealt with when it came to alcohol. I suppose a psychiatrist could have helped with that years ago, but I've never gone to a shrink. Boring people to death with your problems is what good friends are for.

Brian asked me what it was that gave me the strength to quit. I said I didn't really know. He said he thought I just refused to let anything beat me. I refused to let it win. He's probably right. (If only I could apply this logic to my credit card debt.) Watching the part of the movie where Denzel realizes that he's been lying to himself and everyone he knows for his entire life is what sent me over the edge. I finally remembered what I had been blocking for years, what it truly felt like to quit drinking. I had kept so many walls up for so long – putting my brave face on sobriety – but there in the darkness of that theater, over a decade after I quit drinking, it came rushing in like a tidal wave. I suddenly recalled every second of my journey. I did it alone – and it left me raw.

Martin Sheen says people who don't go to AA are just white-knuckling it. Well, I'd love to shove my sober white knuckles up his ass. It doesn't matter how you do it – just do it. Being drunk is a waste of time. I used to think that it was cool to be a drunken writer – like Hemmingway. Then I read some stuff I'd written while I was under the influence, and it would have been a farewell to my career. I never would be where I am today if I still drank.

I don't get up and talk about my drinking to roomfuls of people, and I don't judge people who do. Whatever gets you through it – do it. For me, it's just a part of my past... and I'm past it. I went through it alone – and I go through it alone – and quite honestly I don't even think about it – until I do – and then sometimes I come undone. Even I continue to be stunned by my own will power, but I think the second you realize if you don't stop doing something you will die – you manage to get a handle on it. I have been sober for 14 years now. I have never looked back. I have never once said, "Man, do I need a drink." I just quit. Cold turkey. The end. Story over. I think I've been successful with sobriety because everything got better the second I stopped. It's a testament to what we humans are capable of doing if we put our minds to something. Life for me is too good to be seen through wine goggles. I am not ashamed of my past – I use it to drive me to my future – only now if I get pulled over – I won't go to jail.

It was pretty easy for me to forget most of the dumb things I did while drunk because quite frankly – I didn't remember most of them. These days if I see someone who looks vaguely familiar, I just apologize. When your past is littered with chardonnay and kamikaze shots – this is the easiest response and usually the most necessary. When I run into an old friend who starts a conversation with "Hey, remember the time we blah blah blahed?" I usually just say – "I was drunk." One of the great things about being sober is that you no longer have to make excuses for your dumbass behavior, and you tend to remember everything you do at night because it no longer involves a car accident, the police, and a man in your house wearing an oven mitt on his penis.

However – there are moments in sobriety when you run into someone who seems to have way more information about you than he should – someone who believes you have met, and you have zero recollection of this person. This happened to a girlfriend of mine the other night. Her past is similar to mine, though perhaps slightly less alcohol fueled. A young man came up to her and the following conversation ensued.

Him: "Hey how are you?"
Her: "Uhm, do I know you?"
Him: "Well, I drove you home from the Viceroy last night."
Her: "Uhm, I don't think so. I gotta go."

Now, I know what you're thinking. Why not just set the guy straight? But here's the rub: When you have a past where this kind of shit happened, you think well, it could have happened, right? And so she fled the area with no more questions asked. You just never know.

The biggest issue with this entire scenario for my friend, however, wasn't the fact that she was so drunk she let a total stranger drive her home – it was that she was so drunk she went to a hideous cheesy bar in Los Angeles called The Viceroy, a place she wouldn't step foot in if sober. Was she leading the secret life of a person she herself mocks? What else has she been doing drunk that she doesn't remember? Was she shopping at Ed Hardy? Did she have a French pedicure? Was there suddenly a pair of white pumps in her closet? Did she own a Maltipoo? Will the last place on her GPS be The Olive Garden? After careful analysis and some fairly brilliant deducing, we concluded there could only be one answer – she has a Douchebag Doppelganger. There's some chick out there who looks just like her, but is a complete and utter idiot. *She's* going to cheesy clubs, talking to cheesy men, and letting them drive her home in their BMWs while she taps her fake nails on his dashboard to a Maroon Five CD. It's a terrifying thought, and now a great excuse. I have decided this is my answer to everything from now on. I will no longer apologize for things I've done in my drunken past – I will blame them on that weird chick who looks just like me. I will invent a Douchebag Doppelganger. She will have a tramp stamp, a navel ring, and massive hair extensions. Her name will be Amber, and she will live her life unapologetically.

I do believe however that my love affair with liquor has left me retarded. Not in the mentally deficient kind of way, but in a growth sort of way – as in – my life is in a state of arrested development. I have come to this brilliant conclusion from one conversation with one person, who said he had read somewhere that people who quit drinking revert to the age they were before they started drinking. This would make me 13. This explains why I don't feel like the age I am and I certainly don't act it. I proudly burp out loud, laugh at fart jokes, curse like a sailor, spend beyond my means, leave my dishes piled in the sink, don't hang up my clothes, and find men in their 30s exactly the age I'd like to date. (If only they felt the same way.)

But I think my new-found youth is what led me down a slippery slope, and after 13 years of clean and sober living – I fell off the pure wagon. In a desperate move from a desperate woman living on the verge of a no-sleep breakdown, I took "the pot." I'd like to blame menopause for the lack of sleep, since I blame everything else on it: "I ate birthday cake and Cool Ranch Doritos all day.

Must be the 'pause.'" But the truth of the matter is – I haven't slept in years. Maybe it's the combo-platter peri-menopause to menopause – who knows? I know I never will. I was just hoping some Mary Jane would cure what ailed me. So one day, my young person persona talked to an actual young person who happened to have a prescription for pot. (P.S. Every single solitary person in Los Angeles has one.) He said I should try some mild pot, and that it would help me sleep. Apparently pot now comes in doses – and flavors – and shapes– and sizes. There are standard-issue bags of weed, chocolates, brownies, gummy bears, jolly ranchers, and tea. Leave it to Weed Heads to come up with fun ways to get high. I didn't want to smoke any, since I knew that would lead me back to cigarettes quicker than I could say, "I'll take a pack of Marlboro Lights please." (I still miss smoking. That was a fantastic habit.)

I opted for the mildest form – tea. He went out during our lunch break and scored me three bags of tea – chamomile marijuana. He brought them to me a little white paper bag and slid them across the conference room table like he'd just purchased me a gun with the number filed off. That actually might have been more helpful in my war against sleep. I held on to the tea bags for two days until it was Friday. I figured I'd better wait until the night before a day off in case I had a total drug breakdown and had to be rushed to Betty Ford immediately to get my stomach pumped and my head straight. For two days, it was all I could think about. The excitement was palpable. My addict behavior came screaming back. I don't remember being this excited. I wanted to write a poem to my tea bags. *What would happen to me? How buzzed would I get? Would I crack open a 40 and wash my pot high down?* I may have been clean for 14 years, but the lack of sleep was chasing that care away real fast.

And then, there it was – Friday night. I rushed home from a show taping, broke out one of those puppies, and read the instructions. "Drink ½ dose the first time." So I brewed it up and drank a full dose. Nothing. Nothing. Nothing. An hour later – still nothing. I finally fell asleep the old-fashioned way and woke up a gabillion times during the night like I always do. The pot tea did nothing – until the next day, when in the middle of a Bar Method class, I got a massive headache that felt like my brain was melting and almost barfed mid-plié. I immediately went downtown and scarfed a pile of Greek food. So, I guess I at least got the munchies. It seems the pot tea was a little too mild, and I guess my system is a little too clean to handle foreign substances.

I decided that I was going to have to find yet another way of getting a good night's sleep. "But why give up on weed? There are tons of other ways to ingest it," said a friend who is clearly a pothead. He suggested I get a license and try a few things. This sounded like a fun adventure to me because it involved shopping, and the next day during my lunch hour at work – I got a medical marijuana card. Yep, it was that easy. They should make it a drive-through quite frankly, because I wasn't even out of my car long enough to warrant a parking space. I told the doctor I was having sleep issues, and she told me how wonderful pot was for this. (She might have been high too. In fact, I'm pretty sure everyone is high now.) After 10 seconds with her, I took a lovely picture, and boom! Medical marijuana card – done. I even got to take my picture with my cool fedora on – although that prompted my first pot place to tell me I looked like Indiana Jones. Which, fuck you, I don't.

So, there I was with card in hand and off we went to the Pot Store. I don't know what the legal term is for these places, but let's be frank – they're pot stores – and I love to shop. It was amazing! There are jars of pot everywhere! I live in the coolest place on earth, because you can just walk into an ordinary storefront and walk out with some choice buds! (That's pot talk.) I started with ingestible items, like gummies, some kind of chocolate chew, and even a red velvet cupcake. I got quite the education on what you can eat, and man do they make it fun! I was a kid in a pot candy store. The first night I took one-eighth of the dosage they suggested. It was perfect. I slept like a baby – a very high baby. The second night I tried a bit more and KABAM! I was high as a kite and thought there was a monster in my closet that was going to eat me or stab me or stab me and then eat me. I tried a few other ingestible items, but the problem was – they take too long to get you high, and you never know how high you're going to get.

That's when I decided to take the plunge. It was time to vaporize. Again, this involved a store and shopping, so that was cool. I bought a teeny little vaporizer pipe that cost more than a pair of Manolo Blahniks and a whole bunch of weed. I started with something called LIQUID COKE. The pipe is so cool because it's a "smart" pipe. It lights up when it's hot enough to use and shuts itself down when not in use. It's the iPod of Vaporizers—the" iPot ," I guess you could call it. I got a nice buzz and fell asleep. I went back to the Pot Store to get more, but unfortunately outed myself as an old uncool woman when I asked for the DIET COKE. "You mean liquid coke?" "Uhhhhhh yeah, I was kidding. Pot humor." After that, however, I did become quite the sleep pot connoisseur. I bought TRIPLE KUSH, LIQUID COKE, RED DIAMOND, and LAVENDER. I slept a lot better but forgot the one thing that comes with getting high – the munchies. I don't know what you kids call them today, but that's what we called it back when I first smoked pot in 1843. (I remember when my parents found my bong, and I told them I was keeping it for someone else. Dumb parents.)

So now I had finally found a way to kick back and relax and get some sleep. It seemed not to be addictive at all – but it was turning me into a whale. I was afraid I was going to eat my boobs back to their pre-surgery size, and once again, I was trapped in a moron-like rabbit hole that I didn't know how to climb out of. *Damn you, Mary Jane!!* I decided to do the only sensible thing – take all food out of my house. I wasn't ready to give up on the Wacky Tobacky just yet.

One night, I decided to do something completely crazy. I smoked pot – and left the house. I was freewheeling around Los Angeles with a pill container of weed and a pipe!! I was smoking pot in my car on a dark street like it was 1975. I was thrilled with myself. It was the most fun night I'd had in a long time. I went to a party with my friend Mary, and we laughed at everything and nothing was funny. I made a terrible, horrible discovery – pot made things hilarious – dumb things – all things. I stopped smoking pot alone in my bed and started smoking pot with friends. I recently got high with my friend Brian before dinner at a restaurant and laughed so hard my face hurt. I felt like a kid again. A high happy kid. I went to a concert with my friend Matt and got high and danced around in my leather pants. Then I got really paranoid and thought, *"Oh, my God. I'm an old woman in a club, wearing leather pants like it's some kind of rock outfit, and people are laughing at me."* Then, I laughed at myself. Smoking pot is genius, and it's not just for the cool kids in my neighborhood who wear ski caps when it's 80 degrees.

I wish I had discovered pot when I first quit drinking. It would have made the journey into sobriety a lot easier. I wouldn't have wanted to peel the skin back from my face while screaming and hating everyone I know. Pot does not make you do things you wouldn't normally do. The only thing it's a gateway to is Fritos. I did become a vegan soon after I started smoking pot, and my friend Christian became very concerned. He's gay, and the last thing he wanted to hang around with was some hairy armpit chick who ate tabouleh and wore brand names. I told him I was still wearing Chanel underpants. I heard him breathe a giant sigh of relief.

Chapter Ten

Seize The Gay!

There is nothing I love more than a Super Mary Gay taking someone down. Like a hissing tire going flat, the "S's" are flying, and the person on the other end of their sibilant spew has no idea what's happening and usually just stares into the face of beautiful evil. I think angry gays could make some serious cash if they all got together and formed a company to rent themselves out to boring people who don't know how to handle their shit. I mean, the possibilities of what an angry gay can manage for you – tell your boss to fuck off, demand some respect from your credit card company, or break up with your boyfriend – are endless, though that last one could be dangerous if you have a hot boyfriend and you send in a hot angry gay, and if you live in New York or LA chances are your gay is hot. None of my gay friends in LA are "queen-y." I may have to import one.

I am not one of those girls who believe gay men love women. If they loved us so much, they'd fuck us. Just mention the word "vagina" to a gay man, and watch him back away from you like you're a leper – a leper wearing shoes that he wants. I don't ask gay men to cut my hair, pick out my clothes, or tell me how I look in general – although they always offer opinions on all of these things, especially when they haven't been asked. I'm not saying that gay men don't know about style – of course they do – they just aren't that trustworthy when it comes to you looking hot if the object of your hot-getting outfit is a guy they think is hot too. Gay men believe that all men are about a cocktail away from cock. And quite frankly, they may be right. If I was a dude and some of my hot gay friends approached me, I'd be gay for pay in a heartbeat. But I'm not one of those women who fall in love with my gay friends. Once you tell me you like boys, I'm out. And for those of you keeping count of how many gay men are my friends – take note: If you call me a "fag hag," I believe you should be hit by a bus – immediately. Both words are offensive.

I do think gay men relate more to women because we tend to see the world more like they do – in color and richness and texture – as opposed to straight men – who only see it in black and white and duh. Plus, for the most part, we can't fight over men. There is zero competition and no reason to be jealous. We're just not hunting the same men, and if we were – the gay would win, hands down. Women do not know how to handle sexual warfare the way homosexual men do. It's next-level shit for them. It's an art form.

Just take a look at that website every gay man on the planet seems to know about… Grinder. It alerts you to nearby gays, telling you how many feet you are from one. I loaded the app onto my iPhone because one should always know how close they are to a gay. It was a $2.99 investment – because I got the super upgraded Grinder. (I *am* Jewish. I need the best.) It was $2.99 well spent. Hundreds of snapshots of gays doing all sorts of things popped up. A lot of them were just pictures of guys rubbing their chests. Almost all of them were shirtless. They really should be pant-less. There's a button that says "load more gays." What an option!! *Why don't straight people have this? That's something I could use.* "Load more guys." I love being in a crowded restaurant and my Grinder telling me I am 10 feet from a gay, but the gay doesn't have his picture posted. The whole night can be spent playing "Find the Gay." This is a game all women play anyway in LA, so Grinder just weeds out the ones to steer clear of.

I was standing in front of my house one night, and Grinder told me I was 10 feet from a homosexual. The only other person on my block was my married next-door neighbor getting into his car. I think he was going out for some late night gay. I remember the first time a gay man moved into my neighborhood. I didn't know he was gay at first, because it's hard to tell someone's sexuality from just having your face pressed against the glass in your living room window. I watched him move in and out for about an hour before getting myself dressed and wandering over like a super-creepy straight lady welcome wagon. His name is Christian, and we talked for about five minutes. No sign of gay. No limp wrist. No hissing tire. No comment on my shoes. No clue whatsoever. The straightening of the gay male is really killing my Gaydar.

Then, like gray skies parting and the sun shining through, another male walked out of the house and up to Christian and me.

"Hi, I'm Tyler." I squealed. Literally. Squealed. Me: "Are you a couple?" Them: "Yes, we are." Me: "Yes! (Fist pump) Ohmigod, that's amazing. Gays! Yay!" Pretty sure that's not the response they normally receive. Plus, I could instantly tell that these were "good" gays. The kind that like real food and culture and will most likely improve your neighborhood in some way.

These were gays I could make my own. And I was right. I hit the Gay Lottery.

There are bad gays living here in LA. A lot of them. I think they snuck in from some Midwestern state where no one taught them how to dress or decorate or open restaurants. It's a shame. I would like to institute some type of gay border control – so we only get the chic homosexuals. I also love that there is a whole other culture I get to learn from. For instance, my new neighbor gays taught me the term "otter." I had heard of "bear" and" top" and "bottom" and "Mary" and "Little Debbie" and oh so many others, but "otter" was new to me. According to the *Urban Dictionary*, an "otter" is a gay man who is very hairy all over his body, but smaller in frame than a "bear". Such distinction! That's what I'm talking about. Straight men would never group themselves and if they could it would only be by penis size. Gay men don't need to do this because they already know what every man has in his pants. They have a Stick Sense.

Gay men and straight women can commune on so many subjects – and help each other with an array of predicaments. For instance, a gay friend told me the whole skinny jean thing is causing quite a dilemma for him. He has nowhere to put his wallet, and a simple ChapStick in his pocket makes it look like he's carrying candy – something no right-minded gay man would carry. That is reserved for straight men – who like children. I'm starting to realize that I need more lesbian friends. We also have something in common. We are annoyed by straight men.

They say that straight men can't be best friends with women, but I had a straight best friend for more than 15 years – until he came out. It was pretty devastating, and not because he was gay, but because my Gaydar was so far off I didn't even notice. I mean, I did not have a clue. In fact, he may be just be pretending to be gay so he doesn't have to date me. I'm *that* difficult. He used to have this male friend who was always at his house when I got there and stayed after I'd left for the night. I'd get up to go, and his friend would remain firmly planted on the couch – and I'd think, *"God these guys are fucking retarded"*… but never, *"God these guys are fucking."* I even asked him, "How come he stays so late all the time?", and his response was, "Oh, he's just weird." I am a moron! I mean, if I'd caught them in bed and he'd said, "Oh, we're just making the bed – from the inside," I would have bought it.

Now, it wasn't 1808, it was 2008, and I was well-versed in gay. I just couldn't see it. He finally came out to me after seeing the movie "In Her Shoes." Despite the irony, there was no real tie between the movie and his confession. It was just the timing of it all. We sat outside the theater in silence after it ended. He turned to me with tears in his eyes and said, "There's something I have to tell you." I had never ever seen this man cry.

Me: "What's wrong are you okay?"
Him: "No"
Me: "Do you have cancer?"
Him: "No. It's just that I'll never get married or have kids or do anything normal."
Me: "Are you dying?"
Him: "No I'm… it's Robert." (The friend who was always around)

Me: "Is Robert dying?"
Him: "No he's, we're…"
Me: "Ohmigod you're gay? Is that it?"

He told me he didn't really know what he was, but he was in love with Robert and had been with him as a couple for five years. Five years!! He said they had just broken up because Robert wanted him to come out to me and he simply didn't know how. He thought it would end our friendship. Quite frankly, I was impressed by the magic act he pulled off of keeping Robert a secret. Now there was a point in my life where I _was_ in love with this man, but it was during a time he thought he might still like girls. And this was why he didn't want to tell me the truth. He didn't want me to stop loving him. Which is insane – I just shifted the *way* I love him. It made me really sad that he felt so pained by what was merely the truth of his life. That's what's wrong with this country – no one gets to just relax and be who they are and live out loud and proud. Except for the mental patients – like every news anchor on Fox – they won't shut the fuck up about their opinions.

I think it's disgusting when people ask a guy if he's gay. Unless you have plans to blow him, why do you need to know? No one has ever asked me if I'm heterosexual, and they certainly haven't asked if I like missionary- or doggie- style, so why is it cool to query on whether someone's a "top" or a "bottom"? How will this help you in knowing this person? "Darn, if I'd known you were a 'bottom', I would have made you go get me shit at the store." "Oh, you're a 'top'? I guess you should lead the meeting then." I don't think the policy should be, "Don't ask, don't tell." It should be, "Don't ask, but if someone does ask, DO tell." No one should be ashamed or afraid to admit their sexuality – they should be ashamed to admit they like the feeling of a warm diaper and sipping from a baby bottle at the age of 43. But you can't keep that person quiet – in fact, they have their own TV show. Being angry at someone for who they fall in love with is just insane. How come no one gets upset by those women who write letters to serial killers in prison, then go and marry them and have conjugal visits and give birth to their little devil babies? That's something to protest. If one more person tells me that God created Adam and Eve, not Adam and Steve, I'm going to punch that person in the face. It's not even a good line.

I love all of my gay friends, and not because they're gay – but because they're great friends. My best friend is still my best friend, only now I get to talk to him about everything. It has changed our relationship for the better, and while I'm no longer in love with him – I will never stop loving him. I don't' really understand his sexuality, but then again, I don't understand why a straight man puts his tongue between a girl's legs. I did it once as an experiment, and I still have bad acid flashbacks about it. The bottom line is, you can have great love for something or someone without understanding. Just ask my parents. And if you don't have any gay friends, I suggest you go out and get some immediately, and get the kind that will handle your shit. Christian recently took down a nasty neighbor who walked passed my house every day and said mean awful things about my dogs. He verbally slapped her so badly she hasn't shown her face again. A gay friend understands that a single woman's dogs are her children because for so many of them – that's the

only child this screwed up world will ever let them have.
Seize the gay people. You'll never look back.

Chapter Eleven

If These Dogs Could Talk

You know those annoying people who show you hundreds of pictures of their dogs doing things they believe is adorable and talk about them as if they are their children? I am one of those people. In fact, I may be President of those people.

I had four dogs, which is equivalent to fifteen cats, which is unacceptable in most circles – including my own. I didn't mean to have four dogs, but the oldest one, Zoey, simply refused to die. I used to joke about this all the time until it happened – and then I thought I would never stop crying.

Zoey, the Miniature Pinscher, was – wait for it – 17. If you do the math, that's two billion in human years. She was blind, arthritic, and pooped and peed herself every chance she got. I would spend every morning cleaning both Zoey and the crate she'd decimated. She loved pooping and then stepping in it with the shit oozing through her nails, only to fly off in every direction the second I picked her up because she was freaked out that I was actually some kind of giant chicken hawk flying her to her death and her legs would scramble through the air while she tried to get away. I have been clawed by a poop-filled dog nail more times than I care to admit.

My friends would come over and see her walk into tables and fall down entire flights of steps, and once she even fell out of the house. They would always say, "You should put her down" and give me that look as if I was the one being cruel. I know it's considered insane to compare dogs to people, but if you have a dog, you know what I'm talking about. You can't just pick up a living, breathing thing you've spent almost two decades with and drive her to Doggie Dachau and say, "Get in the shower and breathe in real deep, honey, it's fine", without feeling massive amounts of guilt. I had asked her to die on numerous occasions. The conversation always went something like this. "Zoey, I just don't think we have a quality relationship any longer. You don't like to be picked up or hugged, and you are ruining all of my floors."

Zoey was always nonplussed by this conversation. It's as if she didn't understand me, and I know she did because she was the longest relationship I'd ever had. I could never put her "to sleep," as people like to say. *What if I see her when I get to heaven and she can talk, and she says, "You know, Mom, it was totally fucked up that you killed me." What if, in heaven, dogs and people are even? What if she makes my celestial end a non-living hell because I offed her?*

I know people always say they wish their dogs could talk, but I'm thrilled mine don't. That would, in fact, be hideous. If any of my dogs could talk, I'd have to go into the "Human Protection Program." They have seen some seriously disturbed behavior on my part... especially Zoey, who lived through the height of my drinking. Zoey traveled with me everywhere and even had a little leather bomber jacket with her American Airlines wings on it – although she really didn't deserve those wings because the first time we flew together, she had projectile diarrhea all over the airport. Clean up at Gate 47!! I was horrified. I walked away pretending I knew nothing about it. If Zoey wasn't going to talk about my shit, I certainly wasn't going to rat her out for hers.

Zoey had seen the absolute worst of me and never showed any signs of disloyalty. For that, I could not kill her. Zoey was a survivor and the best friend a girl could ask for. She never said, "You shouldn't have another drink" when I was on my third bottle of wine. She never said "Don't fuck that guy" when she knew he'd never leave his girlfriend, and she certainly never pointed out how truly bad my taste in men was. She never said "You look fat", or "I hate that dress" or "Don't you think that's a bad idea?", or anything negative about anything I was choosing to do. She just wanted a cookie for her silence. This is a concept that should be adopted by humans: "I give you a treat – you shut the fuck up."

When Zoey hit 17, however, she started acting a little differently. She wanted nothing to do with me and would just stand around and stare into a corner all day. I needed to know what was bothering her, so I did what any normal, rational, smart-thinking person would do – I had a doggie psychic come to my house to talk to my dogs. My friend Jeff had a beautiful dog named Casey who wasn't acting like herself. He knew something was wrong with her, but of course Casey couldn't tell him so he found someone Casey could talk to – an "animal communicator" named Star. Things had worked out so well for Jeff and Casey that he and his boyfriend Gage gave me the gift of this psychic and paid for a session for her to come talk to my dogs. My first thought was – *"I'd better hide Zoey, because that bitch will take me down and tell the psychic how mean I am."* I was not that far off. Zoey was the first one who "wanted" to talk to Star. Uh-oh.

- 125 -

The whole process was pretty fascinating. Star would ask me what questions I had for Zoey and write them in a little journal. Then she'd close her eyes and quietly sit. After that she'd open her eyes and write something in the journal, then close her eyes and repeat the process over and over again – for about 20 minutes. I was pretty sure that if I grabbed the journal, it would say, "Found another sucker" over and over again, filling the pages like Jack Nicholson did in "The Shining." But apparently, Star really was having a full-on chat with Zoey, and it wasn't pretty.

Zoey told Star that she didn't understand why I didn't have any compassion for the fact that she was now 100% blind. Didn't I realize that she had lost absolutely everything and how scared she was? Star said, "She hates being picked up because the height is terrifying to her and she loves being quiet and in her crate." *Oh shit, I was in trouble.* She told Star that I would never have to make the gut-wrenching decision to "put her down" and that she knew she was at the end of her days, but also that I would "know" that she was ready to die when she simply stopped eating. I sobbed like a child and have never felt such a deep and horrible guilt.

I know most of you are currently thinking – "Hey, this Heidi is one hell of a gullible lunatic," but here's what Star told me that made me realize she was truly talking to my dogs. Peaches, the French Mastiff, had just started acting really mean to Zoey. She would snap at her whenever she came near, and this was a brand-new behavior. She closed her eyes... asked Peaches why she was being cruel to Zoey – silently of course – and then opened her eyes and looked right at me and said, "Zoey went to the bathroom near Peaches' bowl, and Peaches is pissed off." Holy crap, this was totally true. I was so used to Zoey shitting on every square inch of floor in the house that it never even registered, and I totally forgot it had even happened. Well, Peaches hadn't forgotten; that was for sure. Star wrapped up her session by telling me that animals are here to love us unconditionally and to teach us things. Clearly, Zoey was trying to teach me that I was a terrible mother.

Life went on as usual at my house for the next few weeks. I even took Zoey's crate, which Star said she loved sleeping in, and completely lined it with faux fur. It was a warm and cozy den. She seemed to really enjoy it, until one night I heard her crying and moving about in it. It was like she couldn't get comfortable. I finally took her into bed with me. It was not her favorite place to be those last few years, but I wanted her close to me. That night, I woke up at 2 am to the sounds of Zoey having a massive stroke. It was the beginning of the end, and the end sent me straight to the Porn Convention. I know – not the ending you were expecting.

In case you've never been to the Porn Convention, let me fill you in. It's where all of the creepy people in LA can be found, and I went swimming in their repulsive DNA pool. It was called "Exxxotica." Yes, the three x's should tell you just how grimy it was. This was a place that needed hand-sanitizing stations every five feet. I had to pee while I was there, so I doubled down on the toilet seat covers. I would have been happier if they had hermetically sealed me in something before we started roaming the booths. I'm fine with porn when enjoyed in the privacy of your root cellar where you keep your underage dirt covered girls tied up, but quite frankly this was a little too out loud and proud for me. "Tragic" was the word that kept coming to mind.

I went with my friend Suzanne, and at noon we purchased our $44 tickets. We went inside the brightly-lit room filled with girls, dicks, and a lot of sex toys and not surprisingly, we were the only women at the convention who were not porn stars. Well – us and one woman who was about 6'8" and walked behind her very short boyfriend with her hand on his head. I think I saw a collar and a leash, but I'm not sure. An older gentleman asked to take a picture with us. He probably thought we were retired "xxx" stars and wanted to get a shot with a couple of classics before we died. There were porn stars of every size and shape and age. They played their videos on monitors behind them in their booths as they signed autographs. There was one woman who was far too old to be naked on film, and thankfully she did not have a monitor. I did not want to see her taking it doggy style. I did not want to see her taking it any style.

All the girls were in very skimpy outfits, and of course this led me to do what all women do – look for cellulite. I always feel better when I see cellulite on someone else, and when I see it on a porn star – it's like a super double bonus. Not only are they on a path of destruction; they are also walking there in bad Plexiglass shoes and are covered in cellulite. There were even two girls on a seesaw in creepy baby doll clothing. I had never seen two people look more bored. I felt like I was living inside a Fellini film, complete with midgets. You could take a picture with them if you tipped them and while I desperately wanted one – I didn't have any singles and I wasn't drunk.

Suzanne was looking for a gift for a bridal shower but I found the best booth at the entire convention – a jewelry stand with a crazy old woman selling fake Chanel jewelry. Finally something I could relate to. I guess she was there for all the gross men who'd dragged their girlfriends to the porn convention. I bought two necklaces and a pair of earrings. Suzanne bought me a rainbow cock pop or a "dick on a stick" as it was called, and after about an hour she said, "Do you think you got your $44 worth?" I said, "I got that before we even walked in the door."

I went to the Porn Convention on that balmy Saturday afternoon in LA because I was desperately trying to move through what had been the most horrible morning of my entire life – the death of my best friend. It turns out Zoey had totally lied to that psychic, and I was forced to make that decision she swore I never would – to put her to sleep – or what I believed it really was – killing her. There are very few things that can break me, and I try to find the humor in everything, but suddenly I was crushed so deeply I couldn't see my way through to the other side. I had to say goodbye to one of life's greatest girlfriends and my incredible companion through so many difficult chapters in my life.

It started with that stroke. We had just gone to bed and she seemed so happy and peaceful at first. Then her little body was wracked with a terrible earth-shattering seizure that scared the hell out of me. I rushed her to the vet emergency room. They said they would give her fluids and watch her and figure out what to do in the morning. What they didn't tell me was – this would be her last night alive. If only I had known that, I would have slept there with her. The next morning, I was told they could not stop her pain and that I needed to give her the dignity she deserved and put her to sleep. I crumbled. It was a bullet to my heart. At first, I couldn't even comprehend what they were telling me to do. I was frozen. I called my best friend Brian. "They want me to kill Zoey. What do I do?" He told me that I wasn't killing her, and that I had to let her go. I didn't like this answer at all. I called my sister Wendy, who had just gone through the whole thing herself with her own dog, Lucy. She said, "You are only keeping her alive for yourself. You can't be selfish about this."

I knew they were right, but I just couldn't do it. I stood there shaking and weeping and holding Zoey, who was clearly in such a horrible place, and I knew it was time, but I couldn't let her go. Now I wanted her to speak. Now I would have given anything to hear a little voice. And I guess in her own way she was talking, because she was literally screaming, and if you know anything about dogs – they rarely show signs of pain. Finally I gave them the permission they needed. I hugged Zoey and put my head on her head while the doctor gave her the two shots that gave my best friend some peace. The screaming finally stopped and in a moment, Zoey was gone – along with 17 years of loyal service.

And that's when the guilt rolled over me in a way I didn't know guilt could roll. I stood there screaming "I'm sorry" to my little Miniature Pinscher, sorry for all of the times I had been mean to her these past few months. Sorry that I hadn't understood just how sick she had been. Sorry that I was a terrible mother who used to joke about her dying and was now begging for her to come back. All I could remember was every moment I did not have compassion for my four-legged best friend. All I could remember was every moment I was unkind. I came home and put her crate in the garage and threw away the little pink coat she had been wearing the past few months. I guess I didn't want to be reminded of what a shit head I had been. I could not stop crying. I still break down every time I think about her. (I'm sobbing right now as I write this.) I took her little sweater out of the garbage later that night and washed it and put it on the nightstand next to my bed, and when her ashes finally arrived, I put the coat and a photo of her in the jar from Jonathan Adler that says "Prozac." She always was a little nuts, and I thought this was fitting. I still miss her very much. She was the recorder of so many moments in my life, and her death symbolized the end of an era.

I now have three dogs, which means I live in a fecal war zone. If you took one of those CSI blue lights to my house – there'd be poo residue everywhere. There's Peaches, the French Mastiff; her niece, Tulip; and Lola the 16-year-old Chihuahua. I've already warned Lola that she'd better die in her sleep. These three continue to provide hours of amusement to make up for the tears shed over Zoey. Case in point: a recent trip to the vet, where I was handed a prescription for shame. Yes, I was publicly humiliated when two horrible things happened, and I'm not sure how to deal with the embarrassment.

First of all, if you want to know where all of the mental patients in all of the land are, they are at my vet – talking to their cats. It's always the Cat People, and they are almost always women. The dog owners are slightly nuts, but the Cat Ladies are full-on bonkers. Last night, it was a Cat Lady who called me out in the middle of a crowded waiting room, and then Peaches herself delivered the second red face-inducing blow. The usual

Friday night crowd was gathered at the animal hospital, picking up their various pets or checking them in. Everyone was comparing animal ailments. "Mine has a bad heart." "Mine had a cyst removed." "Mine was in a fight with another dog." Etc. It was like the animal version of that boat scene in "Jaws" or a Jewish retirement village, with everyone trying to top the other in who has the worst injury. In the corner of the room, however, was Crazy Cat Lady. She was chatting it up with her tabby at decibel level 13 and talking on the phone with someone who's apparently deaf. First she got up and bitched out one of the vet assistants. Then she turned her sights on me, whipping around from the counter and yelling to me... "Oh my God, you're wearing your Target Missoni and I'm wearing mine!" She was referring to a designer item I'd fought hard to get at a recent Target sale. She might as well have pointed at me and yelled "murderer." I was stunned. I tried to hide my head behind Peaches' head, but she kept talking. "I love my skirt. I wear it every day. I'm a seller for the most part, but I had to have this skirt for myself."

The entire waiting room was staring at me. Yes, I was wearing what I considered a very chic corduroy car coat I'd picked up. She, however, was wearing the entire Missoni look, top to bottom – and if you're not familiar with Missoni, it's like wearing a kaleidoscope. It was an outfit that should have come with a warning: May cause heart attacks, like a strobe light. The fact that she was now comparing us, as if we were two style icons separated at birth, was the definition of shame. I pride myself on my wardrobe. I don't even like to wear the same thing twice, and here was the Cat lady of Glendale outing me at the vet. I went home and threw that coat right into the garbage.

The other thing that happened – to me – was the surprise diagnosis given to Peaches – herpes. "I'm sorry, what?" I said to the vet. "How did Peaches get herpes?" I had been leaving her out during the day, but I didn't think she'd figured out how to unlock the gate and escape. *Was she out there whoring around the neighborhood making out with dirty dogs while I'd been at work? Was my sweet French Mastiff a French slut?* The doctor told me it was a type of papilloma virus that's not exactly like human herpes, but is the same kind of viral infection. They don't know how dogs get it, but it's very common. I guess if one of us had to get herpes, I'm glad it was Peaches. She doesn't seem at all embarrassed.

I have taken my "kids" in to see the doctor for all kinds of embarrassing things. Like the time Tulip ate my poop. Vomit. Breathe. It's not pretty. It's not funny. It's disgusting and quite frankly unacceptable, but it happened so fast I couldn't stop it. She didn't so much eat it as she did drink around it but you know – what's the difference? Poop water or poop itself – it's a tossup on the disgustometer, and I'm sorry for the vomit-inducing moments I'm causing right now. See, sometimes I forget to flush the toilet. I don't know where this habit comes from, and I think it's truly bizarre behavior, but try as I might, it just keeps happening. I don't think I'll ever forget again –not since I saw my dog's tongue dangerously close to a floater.

I delightedly discovered that Tulip had learned to drink out of the toilet at a friend's house during a dinner party when the host said, "What is that gulping noise?" *"Oh, it's just my dog drinking your disgusting toilet*

water. Maybe for desert we can watch her lick her anus."
But none of this reminded me to flip down the lid, and
now I was sitting in a vet's office asking if eating my
poop would kill my dog. "Dogs eat their own waste for
all kinds of reasons," she said to me. "But mostly it's
just because they can." Wow, if I had a nickel for every
time I heard that. But she didn't understand, and so I was
forced to say it again. "No, Tulip ate *my* poo. *My* shit.
The shit out of *my* ass that was in *my* toilet bowl." A
gray color washed over her face. "Oh," she said. "Well,
that is unusual, but it's not dangerous."

I had to change vets.

Being a dog owner means you get unconditional love
on a daily basis and that is perhaps the most difficult
thing in life to obtain. After Zoey died, we lost two more
members of our family – well, Peaches' family to be
exact – her sisters Jess and Honey – who lived with my
friends. I cannot tell you how devastating both of these
moments were for me – in fact, I couldn't even say
goodbye to Jess because I thought I would break for
good. As for Honey – I miss her on a daily basis. My
only hope is that these three are together, rolling around
in some heaven grass – and talking major shit about us.
I'm thinking about getting Zoey's name tattooed
somewhere on my body – maybe above one of those
claw marks she left behind – as a reminder that she was
here.

Chapter Twelve

I Ink, Therefore I Am

Ever see an 80-year-old woman with a tattoo on her ass that says, "Shut The Fuck Up"? Well thanks to me, in about thirty years – you will.

I got my first tattoo back when it was illegal to get one in New York. Helen Gurley Brown I went together and got a "two-fer." That's a joke, of course. She was way too young. It's hard to believe, but it was not legal to get a tattoo in the city until 1997. Before that, you had to find a "guy." I found my "guy" in his apartment in Brooklyn. His name was Huggy Bear. And the second I laid eyes on him, I should have run for the hills.

I met Huggy Bear back before I realized there were consequences to doing dumb shit like going to a stranger's apartment – consequences like dying and being made into a skin dress. When I look back on some of the shit I pulled back then, it's truly amazing that I'm still alive. I remember the trip to Brooklyn (a place you didn't go unless you were going to that Saturday Night Fever disco) and I remember thinking, *What the fuck am I doing?*" when I first met Mr. Bear. He was huge. He was scary. He was about to stick a needle in me. "What kind of tattoo do you want?" Huggy asked. And that's when I realized, I had zero plan whatsoever for what would happen *after* I found a tattoo guy. I wanted a tattoo so badly, but I hadn't actually given one second's thought to – a tattoo of what? "And where do you want it?" Uh-oh. Stumped again.

I picked a tiny rose with a stem that pierces a heart (let's all say" cliché" together), and I got it on my upper right thigh. Thankfully, the tramp stamp hadn't been invented yet. Huggy asked me if I wanted to see the placement first before making it permanent. "No," I said. "I'm good." (*I'm an idiot*). The process was slightly painful, but it's a pain I've learned is addictive – and I've added eight more to this first one. That's the thing about ink. Once you start, it's kind of hard to stop.

Huggy himself was covered in butterfly tattoos. He said he'd gotten one butterfly for each man he lost in Vietnam. He had over 800. He told me this as he was inking my lame rose. I tried to think of a great story I would tell when people asked me about mine, but I had nothing. Eventually I just paid and ran out. I hated the placement, but what was done, was done. As I added to that rose over the years, I continued to make the same mistakes. I didn't pick before I went, and I never spoke up if I didn't like what was happening. I got another random flower. I don't know why. I don't even like flowers all that much. I got that one in LA before it was legal to be drunk while getting a tattoo. Unfortunately for all of you people with bad tattoos– that law changed too. How's that frog fucking an antelope look now, Drunky? Years later I got another LA tat - a tiny cherub, followed by a purple heart. That last tattoo was the only one that held any meaning for me. I got it because I thought I was being brave for finally moving to LA. A Purple Heart for bravery. Wow, I'm lame.

All of these first tattoos are in one area on my thigh that you can't see unless I'm naked or in a bikini. A tattoo artist once said to me, "You need to branch out." My friend Ann wanted to get a tattoo one night while we were out drunk, but she was a little scared, so I said I'd get one with her. Jesus, it's like I had no concept that they were permanent. She picked this little vine design and we each got one on our right ankle. After it was done I realized it kind of looked like it said S.O.S. This is not a good tat on a girl. Since then, I have added to this design. It now has angel wings. Again, clearly I pick from the "Book of Cliché Designs."

As for that "Shut the Fuck Up" tattoo on my ass, it's actually an island with a palm tree on it, and the island is called St. Fu. It's my island. It's where I go when I want everyone to shut the fuck up, including myself. I also hate the placement of this tattoo.

These days I tend to get ink for my birthday or to mark some sort of special occasion – like Arbor Day – or Look How Good My Hair Came Out Today Day. In the past, I never got anything that was super-visible. All that changed the day I got an "H" on my middle finger. It's super gang-y looking, and once again – I'm not that thrilled with the placement. The only benefit to the "H" is that I can use it to spell "hateful" when I hold it over the "grateful" I had inked onto my left wrist.

I got my last tattoo on my 51st birthday. I knew I wanted to get the tarot card angel "Temperance." This card has come up many times in my psychic readings, and I have been told that he/she is the angel that watches over me. For those of you who are as retarded as I am, the word "temperance" means moderation and total abstinence from alcohol. I decided the best way to have this angel watch over me was to have that angel inked permanently on my body. Since I'd already gone below the elbow, I decided my forearm would be a great spot. I went to a new tattoo parlor because I never went to the same one twice, and I never researched where I went. (Again, something NOT to do if you're getting a tattoo.) They were playing the one kind of music I hate – heavy metal. I had a headache within 15 seconds. This is when most people turn and walk out. I am not most people. The shop owner had massive earrings stretching out his ear lobes. I showed the guy who would be my artist the picture of what I wanted. I handed him the actual Tarot card. If you don't know what they look like – Tarots are very rudimentary drawings. He said, "I'll sketch it up. Come back at 5."

Two hours later, I returned, and he showed me his drawing. It was a sketch of some girl's head, with long flowy hair and two cups floating in front of her face. *Uhhhhh, what?* "What do you think?" he asked, brimming with pride. "I think people will think it's a drawing of my lesbian lover who's a bartender," I said. See pride leave face. Yes, for those of you not paying attention, I told an artist that his work was SHIT. Again, this is the time most people would turn and leave. Again, I am not most people. I explained to him that the actual Tarot was what I wanted and that it held very special meaning to me – as is. He harrumphed, said "fine," sketched out the Tarot, and copied it onto my forearm for me to check placement. See, I was learning. It was massive. It took up my whole forearm. This is not what I wanted. And so I did what any girl who had just insulted a needle-holding artist would do – I said, "It's perfect." And then I sat down and let him put a needle in my arm – actually, quite a few needles.

I left the tattoo parlor and went straight to my birthday dinner at a friend's house. They saw the bandage on my arm. I revealed what I had done. Gasps all around, followed by headshakes and "typical Heidi" comments. Thankfully I now love my Tarot tat. The artist gave me exactly what I'd asked for, and Temperance is now always watching over me. I haven't been back under the needle since. It's been over two years. I want another one, but so many people have tattoos nowadays that the whole thing seems a bit ordinary. And that is the last thing I want to be.

My parents were horrified when I started getting tattoos, and told me that I couldn't be buried in a Jewish cemetery. I thought it was because of the number tattoos Jews got in the death camps, but it isn't. That would have made sense to me. Apparently it has something to do with leaving the earth the way you came in, but I'm already freaked out about laying in a box being eaten by worms, so the whole tattoo ban from a Jewish cemetery isn't that upsetting to me.

People without tattoos definitely judge people with tattoos. If you're a girl with ink, you are somehow deemed rougher and tougher or looser and wilder. This is annoying. Just because I have ink on my ass, doesn't mean my vagina is the Superhighway of Dick. It just means this is the art I have chosen to love and the way I have chosen to display it. My skin is a canvas, and my body is an art gallery. Granted, the art I hung at 20 is very different from the art I buy today, but that's the cool thing about tats. Someone told me that it was a good thing I got the Tarot ink on my forearm so I could wear long sleeves when I was interviewing for jobs. I'm not sure where this person thought I was going to start interviewing, but if you're not going to give me a job because I have a tattoo, then I don't want your job anyway. I'm not in a biker gang. I'm not somebody's

"Old Lady." I mean, I would be if someone would ask, but I'm not. I'm just a girl with some randomly chosen, not- that-well-thought-out tattoos, and for one day, a girl with a nose ring.

I believe the most dangerous emotional state there is - is boredom. I am an alcoholic because I got bored. I once let a homeless man and his dog live with me because I was bored. I had four dogs because I got bored. I have nine tattoos due to boredom, and one day – in a fit of ennui– I pierced my nose. I had been wanting a teeny little diamond to glitter up the nose area – just an elegant little sparkle on my nostril. I had been envisioning it for a while. I decided to finally get the piercing – on Oscar day – in Hollywood. I think it was all the background chatter about beautiful people, and gowns, and who will be wearing whom, and blah blah whatever, that drove me to this piercing parlor called Through The Skin – clever. I went in and immediately saw what I wanted – a teeny tiny diamond. There was no line, they could take me right away, and they didn't laugh in my 53-year-old face and say, "You're nuts." Plus, it was only $50, and *what the hell, why not, let's get 'er done.* Then I was handed a contract. Note to self: If you have to put on your reading glasses to sign the consent forms for a nose piercing, you are too old to get a nose piercing.

Did this stop me? Fuck no. I was taken in back and the piercer put a pen mark on where he wanted to put the earring. Again – out came the reading glasses so I could check. (That's the second sign). It looked good to me – in pen. I lay back. He explained what would happen. And then came the excruciating pain of someone jamming a needle through my nose with zero numbing cream or balm or whatever. Oh. Shit. Because that's what he did.

He just jammed a needle through my nose. Then came the earring. And then came the tears. Yikes. When I got up to look at it, I thought,"Wow – not a good look." I smiled, said I loved it, and left immediately. The second I got in my car, I pulled that diamond booger out. I had a nose piercing for approximately three minutes. Thankfully, it was too soon to leave a permanent hole.

So, for now, I have zero piercings except my ears and nine tattoos. I may not like where some of them are, but it's cool 'cause I think by the time I'm 80, they'll all be in the same place... my ankles.

Chapter 13

Are You There God, It's Me – Jew Hair

I think my three favorite words in the world are "add to cart." If I were one of those Real Housewives, my tag line would be, "I hate to wear the same thing twice, and that's why I'm broke." *Hmmm, maybe I should work on that. Doesn't sound very catchy.* Whenever I have to fill out some stupid form somewhere, I always put down "SHOPPING" as my favorite hobby. I went to London for my 50th birthday just so I could shop uninterrupted in Topshop on Oxford Street for two full days. I spent $4,000. I don't have one single solitary item in my closet from that trip. It's a sickness. I get such a rush when I see something that I like in a store that my heart starts palpitating, and my palms get sweaty, and my breath gets short, and I think, "Omigod, don't let anyone else see that thing I have to have on that hanger before I get to it, and hold it, and touch it, and put it in my bag, and breathe......

"Dear God, please don't let me die before I get to wear these." That's what I say to myself every time I buy a new pair of shoes, which lately seems like every day. I am the old woman who lives in her shoes. Last count – 235 pair, not including boots, but including booties – the greatest creation for those of us who live in warm climates. I believe the person who invented the bootie deserves the Nobel Shoe Prize, if there is one, which there should be. I used to be obsessed with Louboutins, but that phase seems to have ended – I say "seems," because the truth is, it could start again tomorrow. They cost a fortune and are not that comfortable, but every time I see a pair, I hear angels sing. Angels that sound a lot like sales people. Suddenly a beam of light shines down through the store roof and directly onto the shoes as I hold them, mouth open, eyes agog, fingers trembling, credit card burning a hole in my purse. You can see I have a problem. I love shoes. Not flats. Shoes. Shoes with heels, any kind of heel. I do have a few (20) pairs of flats, just in case I break a toe or an ankle or get really skinny (because flats only look good on really skinny people), but for the most part, I like a shoe that says something – like, "Wow, aren't I amazing." Or "Holy shit, do you see me?" Or "Hey, look down here, and not at the wrinkled neck on the crazy lady directly above me."

I believe that a nice shoe can brighten up any outfit. A good shoe can take a T-shirt from Target and turn it into a "look." It's like the furniture in your house. You can buy a cheap couch if you dress it up with a more expensive lamp and coffee table. I am that cheap couch. If someone wanted to get me a great birthday present, they would take me to the shoe department at Saks and let me pick out any pair I wanted. My idea of "fuck you" money is closing down Prada and Miu Miu and taking one of everything in the shoe department. When the Barneys shoe sale is on, I will kill a person at the shoe rack if they touch something I had my eye on. It's a problem, and there is no 12-step program.

Just yesterday, I came to a horrifying realization about my life: I am a hoarder. I have six closets in my house and I use all of them. If you come to visit me – I breathe a sigh of relief if you like living out of your suitcase because there certainly isn't anywhere to hang your clothes. The problem is, I don't like to throw things out because the second I do – it seems I want them again. Despite the fact that I haven't remembered I *had* high-waisted leather floral pants for the past six years, the second I toss them, I remember I had them – and go looking for them – and crumble in a heap that I no longer have high-waisted leather floral pants. *Where the fuck are those high- waisted floral pants?* Sometimes I have the foresight to keep an item. I have found a fur vest from 1989, a dress from when I lived in New York City 16 years ago, and at least three tops I think I owned before I had pubic hair.

Let's not even get into the different sizes I have in everything. I could easily open a store in my home. My friend recently told me my main closet looks like Barneys. Notice I said, "main closet." People always tell me to sell my stuff on eBay, but who has that kind of time? I just throw everything in a garbage bag and put it in front of my house. This way the homeless people in my 'hood get free clothes, and quite frankly nothing would please me more than to see one of my old skirts peaking out of a box on the street.

I also cut the labels out of almost everything I own, from towels to T-shirts. I hate the feeling of a tag on my skin when I'm trying to dry off after a shower or on the back of my neck when I'm wearing a shirt. Besides, when the tag says Forever 21 – who really cares – and who really needs to know? I call clothing items from stores like this – disposable. Want to wear the new Navajo look? Spend $10, not $1,000. You won't feel so badly about seeing the same serape the Pace Salsa guy wears hanging in your closet a week after you buy it if you only paid $10 for it. If you're going to hop on the fur vest trend, then get one for $20. Sure, it'll look like you went out and killed your own coyote before sewing it up into a boxy Daniel Boone vest, but hey – walk fast and no one will ever know. I do not penny-pinch when it comes to shoes and handbags. I could save a small country on what's happening in my shoe closet.

One thing I never remove from clothing – a designer label. Those things can scratch the shit out of me, but I don't care – I worked hard for that rash. That's why they invented cortisone cream. Not only do I proudly display a designer label, but I will tell you who made it the second you compliment it. It's the Jewish law. Example: "Hey Heidi, I love that dress." "Thank you. Versace." If it's something that was acquired at a discount, then the conversation goes something like this, "Hey Heidi. I love that dress." "Thank you. Versace. Seventy percent off." People always ask me, "Why do you tell everyone that you got it on sale?" Well, it's not that I want to – it's that I *have* to. It's also part of being Jewish. I think it may be written in the Torah. "On the seventh day God said – reveal all bargains."

The worst thing that ever happened to me in the whole wide world was the invention of online shopping. My house is like Christmas every day. I love coming home to packages, and because I'm single I don't have to hide my purchases. I have a friend I go shopping with who makes me keep her purchases in my trunk if her husband is home when we return from raping and pillaging the outlet malls. As if we're making a drug drop, we then have to figure out a time we can make the switch and she can take her stuff home when he won't be there, so she doesn't have to explain why she just bought her 65th long black skirt. (She needed it, of course.) She is a very powerful businesswoman who makes her own money. I find this whole thing hilarious. The only person I have to lie to about my purchases is me. Every time I buy something new I say, "This is it – no more shopping for a month." I say that every day. Sometimes twice. People love to tell me that I'm shopping because I'm trying to fill some hole in my life. They're right. I am. But the hole is in my closet, and it's screaming for new skinny jeans and a nice platform shoe from Gucci. I love new things, and not getting something I want is so painful, I feel like I'm going to die. The problem is – I am going to die – broke – surrounded by shoes and quite a collection of skirts, blazers, coats, T-shirts, and about 30 pairs of jeans.

The saddest thing about getting older is that my precious shoe money is now being spent on the maintenance of me. So many things are changing as I get older, and the upkeep costs are starting to rival my mortgage payment. There's hair coloring, cutting and styling; facials; manicures; pedicures; waxing; trainers; skinny clothes; fat clothes; skinny clothes; fat clothes, bloat clothes (which are just slightly bigger than skinny clothes and slightly smaller than fat clothes) –I just can't keep up. Boys have it a lot easier. They just get up and leave the house. There are those who spend a lot of time on their appearance and have more products than I do, and I know we coined a cute word for them back in 1994, but if you're calling yourself "metrosexual," call me after you give your first blow job, because really that's how far you are away from being gay. If you meet a guy who calls himself "metrosexual," there is also a good chance he is from my tribe. Jews like products. Even our boy Jews. So, Jewish or gay? Hard to tell. Very rarely are they both. Even gay men find Jewish men a little too gay.

There are some things I can change and some I can't, and the one thing that is unalterable is my "Jew Hair." I think I spend the most money trying to undo the Jew. I want straight hair. I want long, flowing, shiny, bouncy hair. I want to whip it around like a horse tail, and have it air dry stick-straight when I get out of the shower. I want to feel it on my back and never, ever have to take a styling tool to it. I want to be in a Pantene commercial. I want to complain that I can't do a thing with my hair because it's just too darn straight. The bottom line is, I want Asian hair. If you want to know the true meaning of sacrilege, watch an Asian woman get a perm. This is thumbing your nose at the Hair God, and I know there is one because when I was little, he passed right over my house and put a big red smiley face on all the Asian front doors. Perms on Asian women should be illegal, and the penalty should be a hair transplant with a Jew.

I've been wrapping my hair around a Coke can to keep it straight since I was a little girl at Camp Indian Head. Well, the Coke can is gone, but I still wrap up my hair at night in a truly bizarre fashion to keep it straight. It is the opposite of sexy. It is a male repellent. I believe this is another reason why I don't have sleepovers. Having straight hair in the morning is more important to me than having sex. I have singed myself with a flat iron so many times that if you connect the dots of the burns on my upper body, you get the shape of Idaho. I'm going to start telling people that I have an abusive boyfriend who puts his cigarettes out on me. Hooking up with a beater sounds a little less pathetic than I can't use the same hot stick my 13-year-old niece could master.

Sometimes I like a little curl in my hair, but in order to get this look, I have to blow-dry my hair straight, flat-iron it, and then use a curling iron. I'm pretty sure this is what hell looks like. I am addicted to my curling iron. It is a dependency more powerful than my love of liquor and my daily desire for a Marlboro light. It is a habit so powerful, I don't know if I'll ever be able to shake it. I have been told that my iron is murdering my hair. I have been promised that if I give up my curling iron, I will have long silky hair within one year. This is a long time to wait for something to come to fruition – especially for someone like me. I am Captain Immediate Gratification. I don't wait. I want to join C.I.A. – Curling Iron Anonymous – but it doesn't exist yet. Maybe I should start holding meetings in my garage. I can't be the only curling iron addict out there. In the hierarchy of inanimate objects I would marry – my curling iron beats my Nespresso every time – and that's deep. I have three curling irons, and they are all hanging in a row staring at me – calling to me – begging for me to use them and fix the untamed disaster on the top of my head. I want to put them away, but I'm afraid they'll stage a coup in the middle of the night and escape from the bathroom cabinet and do my hair while I'm sleeping, click-clacking the frizz out of my hair.

It makes sense that a curling iron is killing my hair. It's the same concept as laying my head down on an ironing board and using my Kenmore Steam Pro to smooth out the frizz. I think that's actually how women used to do their hair back in the day anyway. It seems that I need help giving up this addiction, so I have decided to attack my curling iron addiction the twelve-step way:

1. Admit we are powerless over our addiction —that our lives had become unmanageable.
Actually it's my hair that's unmanageable, and my addiction helps. Skip this step.
2. Come to believe that a Power greater than ourselves could restore us to sanity.
Are you there God? It's me, Jew Hair.
3. Make a searching and fearless moral inventory of ourselves.
That's not gonna happen. I don't have that kind of time.
4. Make a list of all persons we have harmed, and become willing to make amends to them all.
How about if I make a list of all the people who will be harmed by the sight of my hair without the curling iron?
5. Make direct amends to such people wherever possible, except when to do so would injure them or others.
Who has this kind of time?
6. Continue to take personal inventory and when we are wrong, promptly admit it.
This is not going to happen. I needed to find another solution. And I did.

Me: "I just got the most amazing Brazilian Blowout, and my hair is super sleek and shiny."

My sister Wendy: "I thought those blowouts give you cancer and brain tumors."

Me: "Uh-oh.

Rule Number One when getting something wacky done to your hair: Read some research – before you do it. Oops, too late. So after my sister informed me about the "cancer" portion of my hair-straightening process, I went online and did a little reading. *She can't be right. There has to be some mistake. How could something so wonderful kill me?* Four hundred thousand death articles later, I realized I may have made a teensy tiny mistake. Here's what one article said: "The popular hair-straightening brand, Brazilian Blowout Acai Professional Smoothing Solution (yep, that's the one I had) contains liquid methylene glycol. When heated with a blow dryer, the liquid releases carcinogenic formaldehyde vapors into the air. People exposed to large amounts of formaldehyde in their professions are at an increased risk for lymphoma, leukemia, and brain cancer." *Well, that doesn't sound good at all. How could this be possible? Do I want straight hair at the risk of cancer? Am I willing to have a tumor the size of a grapefruit? Do I want to breathe in carcinogens every time I blow dry my silky smooth hair?* The answer is YES!

Sadly, the pain of Jew Hair in the summer is really hard to deal with. Why is everything I enjoy in life bad for me? I like sunbathing – cancer. I enjoy sugar – cancer. I have a high-stress job – cancer. What's the point of this crazy life filled with magical distractions if all of them are going to give me cancer? If I find out that going to the movies and watching television are cancerous – I'm chucking it all and buying a pack of cigarettes immediately. I can't even get the new kind of gel manicure anymore, because that's also giving me skin cancer. Quit inventing amazing shit that's murdering me!! How can I be pretty if everything leads to death?

Apparently, the FDA forced these Acai people to make some changes to their product, and the kind I got is actually called "ZERO" and is completely safe. My hairdresser told me that the whole system is really just dangerous to the stylists breathing it every day, so I thanked him for taking the cancer bullet to give me what I want most in life - straight hair. I really appreciate it. But as much as I hate the curly frizz ball that sits atop my increasingly wrinkly neck – I'm still thrilled to have it. Women losing the hair on their heads as they age has to be the biggest fuck up on God's part. I can see how confusing it would have been when he was handing shit out on his cloud that day six billion light years ago, and said, "Okay, here we go – let's separate women from men:

Women – You will bleed from your vagina every month for decades.
Men – You will have things shoot out of your penis for fun for the rest of your lives.
Women – You will gain weight just looking at food.
Men – You will eat whatever you want until the age of 50.
Women – You will fall in love, carry the children, and give birth.
Men – You will have the ability to think with your penis until it has sex with someone other than your wife, and then you will say it has a mind of its own.
Women – You will develop fatty tissue.
Men – You will maintain a nice amount of muscle from watching sports.
Both Of You – You will grow hair everywhere but on women, it will not be considered attractive.

The last one is when God probably said, "Hmmm....
seems the men are getting the leg up on this one. What
to do, what to do? I know – I'll make men lose the hair
on their head." Shazaaam. "Oops, I think I zapped both
sexes." The bottom line is, if you have good hair – people
take notice. Just this morning, John, my homeless friend
who I see every day when I get off the highway, asked
me if I'd changed my hair color. "As a matter of fact,
John, I just had some highlights put in. Thank you for
noticing." Not one of my friends had said a word about
my hair. I am now looking at John in a whole new light.
Perhaps a little makeover could make him the perfect
date. I always know where he is, and I'm already paying
him. John once went missing for a couple of days, and
when he returned I asked him where he'd been. He said,
"voting." John may be dentally challenged – but he cares
about his country. You know, the one that lets him sleep
on the street.

People always tell me they don't give homeless
people money because they are just going to use it to buy
drugs or liquor. This is a ridiculous thought. If anyone
deserves a drink or a nice hit of Oxycontin – it's a
homeless person. They're living outdoors for fuck's sake.
Stop judging people who don't even have a bed. I give
John money for one simple reason. He likes my hair. And
if I ever find out he can swing a hammer – we're walking
down the aisle.

Chapter Fourteen

Home Shit Home

Me: "Hi Marvin; it's Heidi. There's water pouring out of some pipe in my yard. What do I do?"

Marvin: "Is it your water?"

Me: "I don't know."

Marvin: "Did you shut off the main water?"

Me: "Where's that?"

Marvin: "It's in the front of the house by the street."

Me: "I don't think I should do that. I think you should do that."

This is how conversations usually go between me and the main man in my life--Marvin, my gardener. Thankfully, Marvin is a lot more than a flower-planter. He's an electrician, a plumber, a landscaper, a contractor, and anything else I want him to be – unless I want a licensed person for any of these jobs, because Marvin does not come with the State of California's approval. I'm not even sure Marvin is legally allowed in the State of California, but I'm not asking any questions, because without him my life is over.

Every time I need anything done, I call Marvin. I have no idea where he lives, and I don't care how far he has to travel to get to me. Just get here fast – 'cause shit is going down. Marvin only charges me $50 to do just about anything. I have graciously given Marvin to other people because that's how I got him, but I worry that he'll be too busy for me and I secretly want to stop recommending him. I gave him to a friend once, who gave him to Kathy Griffin, and the next thing I knew Marvin was on television renovating her house.

Marvin is the master of my domain. There is nothing he doesn't know how to build or fix. Marvin has climbed through rat poop to find out what smelled in my crawl space. If Marvin didn't bathe in some kind of Paco Rabane cologne, I'd marry him.

Owning a home is a hard thing for a single gal – especially one who doesn't even have a grasp of what owning a home means. I have a ton of paperwork that says this property is mine, but I have no idea what any of it means. I recently had a chat with someone in India who told me my mortgage was going up $300 a month because I didn't have enough money in my escrow account. Umm, what's that? I tried to listen to him explain, but I couldn't understand a word he said. And quite honestly, when I hear an Indian accent I think of 7-11s, and New York taxicabs; and hear Bollywood music, and before I know it, I'm saying "thanks" and hanging up. Owning a home, however, has led me to understand why women get husbands, because it seems there are things that men simply know how to do. I think they get an instruction manual with each nut sack, and it says, "If you don't know how to fix something, fake it. You're a dude, Dude. It's your job." How else can you explain that all men know how to change a tire? Well, almost all men.

But not everything in life can be handled by a handyman. Sometimes you have to call in an expert, and if there's one thing I've found out as a 50-plus single lady, it's that there's an expert for everything. The strange part is, letting these experts into your home when you're alone can be creepy – and by creepy, I mean – I should get a gun. Just the other day, the guy from Closet World said, "If there's anything you need done that doesn't involve closets – I'm good for that, too." *Ew. What the fuck does that mean?* I didn't even have makeup on, so this guy was a real sicko.

If you really want to see a small Jewish woman go on an illegal killing rampage, give her a bee invasion – in her kitchen – 20 minutes before she has to leave the house for a party. Yesterday I entered my kitchen to see one bee, then another, then two more, then six more. Then the screaming began – mine. I called a straight male friend. (Sometimes you have to.) He said, "Turn the lights on. They'll leave!" I did. They quadrupled. They were everywhere. My kitchen sounded like a chainsaw testing facility. I whipped out my handy fly swatter – I have three – and started killing the fuck out of these fuckers. They were flying in through the recessed light fixtures in my kitchen. (Please pause for a moment and admire that I have recessed lighting in my kitchen.) It seemed the lights were now making them multiply and making them even angrier.

Then my producer skills kicked in. I Googled bees and found - The Bee Guy. Clearly they started to think of a more creative name and just said – "Fuck it – go with what you know." Now I understand that bees are endangered, and there may be some new law against killing them, but when you see 50 in your kitchen very close to your dogs, who think catching them in their mouths is sport – you become a murderer. The dilemma was – *How do I swat and apply mascara and false eyelashes at the same time?* I locked all the dogs in my bedroom and continued to murder innocent honey-makers. I texted my friend Becky to let her know I was running late – I had a massive infestation of bees and was freaking out. Her first response: "Let's make some honey!!!" I replied, "It's like a horror movie in here." She fired back, "New band name. Peaches and the Bees."

Clearly Becky is a nature lover and didn't understand that I was losing my mind and living inside a hive. She then said, "At least bees are good, and it's not wasps." I almost jabbed my blush brush in my eye. *Blah, blah, fuck bees and their extinction and their honey-making prowess – THEY'RE IN MY HOUSE BY THE GABILLION PEOPLE!!!! And breathe.* Finally, the bee guy showed up. He put on his little bee hat and checked the area. No swarm yet – just a bunch of bees finding a nice place to start a nest. "Good thing you called now," the bee man said. "If they'd built a hive, we'd have had to take part of your roof off to get to them. By the way – you smell really nice, Ma'am." There's the creepy. $250 I didn't have later, the bee situation was under control. I walked outside to see my neighbor Christian and told him what had just happened. His response: "Omigod, that's horrible.' Exactly, Christian. So the moral of this bee tale is, if you want the right response – tell a gay.

A bee infestation is really nothing compared to the critter whose ass sack sprays cancer juice. I'm talking about skunks. Recently Peaches had a throwdown with a black and white Pepe Le Pew that must have rivaled a WWE match. I didn't see it. But I most definitely smelled it. There I was, sitting at my computer and minding my own business at 5 am, when all of a sudden I smelled something – foul. My office is on the bottom floor of a four-level house. The smell was slow at first, but before I knew, it the stench was so ripe my eyes started watering. *What the hell was that wretched odor?*

The answer: Peaches. My 120 -pound French Mastiff raced down the stairs and over to me, and I thought I was going to pass out. She was bleeding from her nose. And that's when I realized what had happened. Peaches had been sprayed square in the face. I panicked. *I must control the smell now!* I ran upstairs, only to realize I hadn't been Peaches' first stop. She had raced throughout the entire house, burying her skunk-smelling face and body into every surface she could find. The couch, my bed, even the dish towels all stank of skunk. If you've never smelled the odor when it's off the skunk and in your house – it's paint-peeling. I did what any rational thinking person would do. I locked Peaches in a crate, lit every candle I owned, and left for work. Then I called the Skunk Man.

What appeared at my door later that day is the kind of stuff that fuels romance novels and porn websites featuring handyman smut. This guy was hot. Supermodel hot. My very first thought was – *Can I date a man who traps skunks for a living?* The answer was *"yes."* Sadly, Skunk Man was married, so it seems some other woman had asked herself that question way before I did. The hot Skunk Man gave me some magic goop that's supposed to suck all the skunk scent out of your house, and Peaches went for a bath. My house smelled for a month, and I'm convinced that little stinker gave me a tumor or cancer or all of the above; I'm not sure yet. The whole ordeal has really just made me jealous of skunks because, God knows I would love to have a double anus sack that shoots deadly hideous smelling shit onto people. Who needs a gun, when you can just "skunk" somebody? Every time you have a little trouble at work with an office bully – just drop your pants, bend over – and point and shoot.

Something's always going wrong when you're a homeowner, and it seems like everything costs $500 to fix. Unless you have homeowner's insurance—and then it costs $40, but takes six months. My worst nightmare happened on Thanksgiving. While most people were basking in the pre-holiday glow of supermarket light bulbs, I was waiting for repairmen of all shapes and sizes. I was finally home during the week, on a business day, when someone could come to my home and fix things between the hours of 10 am and whenever the fuck they felt like showing up. First up, the Cable Guy. I had moved a box and television set from one room to another – and hoped it would miraculously come back to life. I had returned it to a room it had already been in, so I figured the cable wire was still live. After two days of screwing with it – I had to do the unthinkable... call Time Warner. Cable Man's first question: "Where does the cable come into the house?" Answer: "Isn't that your job to know?" For the next hour he asked me stupid questions, and I answered, getting increasingly annoyed.

Q: "There are five cable lines coming into your home. Which one is which?"
A: "Perhaps the cable man before you should have fucking labeled them?"
Q: "Where did you get your cable modem?"
A: "It's seven years old. No idea. Do you remember where you bought everything you own?"

Eventually, we both realized that the reason the cable wasn't working was because I'd hooked it up to the wrong outlet. Oopsie. There were two cables coming into the room. Once again, a problem was solved by undoing Stupid Girl Logic. I find that the second you yell at someone, you will be the one proven to be an asshole. It hasn't stopped me yet, but I like to keep hope alive.

Up next: the Oven, Freezer, Washer Repair Guy. All three were having issues. My oven had been "door locked" for six months. My *(what's the non- bourgeois name for maid?)* cleaning woman had done something to it and locked it. I have two ovens, a large one and a small convection oven. I'd been using the small one because it's just me, and I don't need the giant one on a daily basis to warm up tofu chicken nuggets. I finally had a day off when the guy could come, and I needed to cook some items for the Thanksgiving dinner party I was attending, so I was killing two birds with one wrench. After two hours and a lot of Russian curse words from Igor – yes, that was his name – I went back into the kitchen to find my entire stove taken apart like a car – bits and bobs all over the floor – and the oven door lock light – still on. He looked at me and said, "Today, you no cook turkey." Perfect. Now I had no stove. Apparently my $10 billion GE Monogram range needs a special technician to come "unlock" it. (So does my vagina, what a coinkydink.) I told him that if he didn't get at least the convection oven back on, he would be fixing ovens in Siberia. Well, I said something like that. After another two hours, it was back to where it had started.

Up next, my freezer. I'd defrosted it twice, but it still jammed up with ice the second I turned it back on. Again, it's a Monogram series – $5 billion – and I can't figure out how to work it. Igor's solution? Unplug it and leave the doors open for 72 hours. Perfect. Thanksgiving is a great time to ruin hundreds of dollars of food items in the fridge. Finally, my washer hose had been leaking. I sent him to the laundry room. Once again, a slew of Russian curses and then a blood-curdling girl scream that made me think he'd found a body. He hadn't. He'd found tons of bodies. Rat bodies… or at least what rat bodies do when they get inside a washer. "You have mouse or rat – it build nest," he said, pointing out all this stuffing-like crap that was pulled apart and laying in the bottom of the washer. After a few more curses, "harrumphs," and sighs. he pulled out all the stuffing. (I gave the pussy some kitchen gloves.) The whole thing was like having Boris and Natasha fix my appliances.

At the end of the day, I'm thrilled I own my own home. It makes life a lot easier when you don't have to explain to a landlord that your dog put her paw through a window (or two) or why your patio is suddenly painted hot pink (a crafting accident), and you don't have to get anyone's approval when you want to cut a hole in the side of your house that a small person (or me when I lost my keys) can climb through (extra-large dog door).

I don't always call something with balls to take care of something I think a vagina can fix. Sometimes, I actually fend for myself. I once put dimmer switches on all the lights in my house. I was so proud of this accomplishment that I threw myself a party. Then I turned the lights down real low as I poured myself a fake beer.

I have a tool box. I have a ladder. I have three different saws. I have a power drill. Granted, none of these things can hug me. But I bet I can call an expert for that.

Chapter Fifteen

Tech Time

Here's the thing about the Internet – everyone has something to say. Here's the thing about me – I don't give a shit. Don't get me wrong, I love a good Google search. In fact, I'm a Google-holic. I will put anything in that "search" box. Long rambling questions are my favorite, and Google always has an answer. Last night at 2 am, I typed in, "Can you die from swallowing gum?" because I'd fallen asleep with a piece in my mouth. I also Googled "how to Heimlich yourself" because after the gum incident, I'm convinced I'm going to die in my home alone choking on something I'm eating in bed in the middle of the night, and my dogs will eat my face when I'm dead. I have to clear my history every morning, because if I do die in the morning after choking on a bag of chocolate chip morsels, I don't want anyone finding my iPad and seeing the embarrassing things I've searched for. I also don't want anyone to find my vibrators – but my niece Amy told me she'd do a clean sweep of my house after I'm gone and get rid of them all. I used to throw my vibrators out before going on a vacation, but that started to get really expensive. I don't even know why I have any sex toys – I'm even bored having sex with myself.

The Internet, however, is allowing us to raise a generation of narcissists. Between Facebook, Twitter, and Instagram, everyone is obsessed with being liked –

and not in the way they should be liked, for being a good person who does good things. No, people want to be "liked" as in – like this picture or this status update or this brilliantly composed 140-character statement. We're so busy telling everyone everything, but it's actually the opposite of connecting with people – face to face – with a conversation. I don't know why they call it "social media." It's the most anti-social behavior there is. One day, no one will ever have to leave the house, which at this point might be a good thing because I can finally gain all the weight I want, and start slugging back martinis and smoking. If no one can see me... no one will know.

I use all three of these social media apps. It's a good way to write my really important thoughts like "I had quinoa for dinner" and post pictures of my dogs. However, I don't care how many "likes" I have. For me, it's a cathartic writing process. The Internet is my shrink. I don't need an appointment, and she doesn't take the entire month of August off. If I write it down and click "send", or "post", or whatever, I'm done with that thought. I say a whole lotta things I probably shouldn't – i.e., everything in this book – and so does everyone else – which makes it really easy to separate the kind of people you want to remain friends with and those you should cut out of your life like a cancer. Just "unfriend" someone. God, if only life were this easy: "You are an asshole, and your thoughts are dumb." Click "remove friend." Never see them again. In fact, wouldn't it be amazing if you could click "remove friend" and that person actually disappeared from the face of the earth!!?? Actually, I probably would have been zapped long ago, so let's not make that a reality.

But Facebook has allowed me to unearth the batshit crazy side of many people I know. For instance, a friend posted this on his Facebook page today: IF YOU TELL THE TRUTH, IT BECOMES A PART OF YOUR PAST. IF YOU LIE, IT BECOMES A PART OF YOUR FUTURE. Blah, blah, delete. I am a firm believer in telling the truth about yourself, and not using it as a weapon against others. But people love to use the truth as a kind of excuse to let their filter fly off the handle. "Hey, I'm just telling you the truth." *I have an idea – if I didn't ask you to tell me the truth – don't. Please keep it to yourself. Your opinion is best used on you. I don't like you enough to care what you think about me, because if I did I would have asked for your opinion, and if I didn't ask for it then I'm clearly not ready to hear what it is you must tell me about myself that is crushing your soul unless you get it out.* I think this statement should be modified to say, "If someone tells you the truth and you didn't ask for it – you have free reign to tell them the truth right back." Like this:

"I liked your hair better long."
"Thank you. But I wouldn't let my dog take style tips from you."

"You really are too thin."
"You're just jealous because you're a fatty."

"I think you should have kept the Porsche."
"I think you should have made my car payments for me."

"Ewww, I'm not a fan of kale." (as I'm eating a kale salad)

"I'm not a fan of you. Shut up. Go away." Click. Remove friend.

But I'm starting to get really scared about the future... technologically speaking. I realize that the older I get, the more my conversations start with – "God, I miss..." Things like the joy of Hawaiian Punch; getting called in for dinner from your outside play; and when you were truly, truly lucky, that dinner being a TV dinner that you got to eat in front of your favorite show while the corn area seeped into the hot chocolate pudding area and the tater-tot section. Oh, it was so simple then. But just the other night, I said those eight little words that when strung together suddenly made me the star of my own episode of "Little House on The Prairie" – lecturing some young kids about having to walk to school with bare feet through the snow for eight hours. The words? "WHEN I WAS YOUR AGE, WE DIDN'T HAVE"... Boom. And instantly, I was old. I'm sure people with kids find themselves saying this all the time, but I don't have kids – I hang out with kids – and I thought we were all on the same page until I outed myself as "The Old One." I love being with twenty-somethings – smart twenty-somethings – as often as possible. They – unlike people my age – are alive – and unfiltered – and curious – and, I believe, keep people my age – alive and unfiltered and curious. (Though let's be realistic – I didn't come with a filter to begin with. They are not – as believed to be – factory-installed.)

I pride myself on staying current about certain things – not because I'm trying to cheat my age or hide it, but because I like to learn about things I didn't know about, and I eat new information about people and places and style and technology voraciously. I don't try to stay "in the know" because I want to be a cool kid – I just don't want to wake up on the couch one day buried underneath a pile of manuals and remotes and not be able to use half the things in my house because I'm too old. Sure, it took the Geek Squad three trips to my place to show me how to use my new TV, but I've got it together now everyone, so lets just calm the fuck down.

But there I was, on my roof deck, with three twenty-something- year-old men – eat your hearts out ladies – when we started talking about cell phones – and I said it. "When I was your age we didn't have cell phones." They looked at me like I'd said – "When I was your age, we used to shit in the street." But it was true. I remember my first cell phone – it was the size of a shoe – and heavier than one – and I thought I was the coolest kid in the world. It was a gray Motorola flip phone, and it was fatter than a gyro. It was probably emanating more cancer than an x-ray machine, but I loved it. I think I was already 30 years old when I got it. I've gone on to have quite a few since then – settling now on an iPhone, which most women my age can't use and when I hear myself saying – "Wait – how do I take a picture?", I'm throwing this thing out.

Once the guys got past how incredibly ancient I am, we started talking about what it will be that they say when they're my age to someone in their twenties that will start with the words – "When I was your age we didn't have" ...Flying cars? Transporting? We couldn't settle on what it was, but I realize that it will be technological – and it will probably make us more alone

– and it will probably be a completely virtual world since we're wrecking the one we currently live in. So for now, I'm going to enjoy my nights with young people – gathered in the current world – where I tell them about the good old days of mimeographing and pay phones. I know I said those eight words, but I don't think they'll kick me out of their club – yet.

One thing I do know that perturbs all people my age when it comes to computers and running our daily lives technologically is passwords. I have about 1,700, and thanks to the various companies, they are all different. Sometimes it's all letters; sometimes it's numbers and letters. Sometimes it's upper case only, then lower case with just one upper case, then one number and one letter and one exclamation point and if you can use that Spanish squiggly thing that works too and ohmigod I can't remember these things. My passwords are all some sort of variation of a place I've never been to, but is fairly easy to remember, and then I do have some written down on my computer, but there are scads I have no clue about. I love when you think you are logging in somewhere for the first time, and you go to register, and it tells you "That email address already exists in our system" and I think – "*Fuck, I must be up at night logging in and buying things, because I sure don't remember joining the Barbecue Sauce of The Month Club.*" That's when I use my "other" email address. The one that's registered to my dead dog – you know, just in case. But it's those passwords and not remembering them that get me every time. That's when you get to play the quiz with these companies, answering the "personal question" you chose to answer if you got into a really difficult password situation. It's like fucking Jeopardy at my house every day. What was your first dog's name? *Uhm, shit, did I say my first dog as a child or my first dog as an adult. Zoe? Or was it Zoey? Or was it Chips? Did I live on Melrose Place, or did they not accept the "Place" part and I had to say just "Melrose"? Fuck, I just want to buy some discreet pee panty liners. Why are you making me take a test!!??* My friend Dan said getting back into his online issue of *Consumer Reports* was like breaking into the Pentagon. All I know is this: If you steal my identity, good luck – every card is maxed out – and quite frankly if you can figure out my codes, I'll be glad to buy you a nice jar of barbecue sauce.

There is a site for everything on the web. People are obsessed with this Pinterest thing. It's basically an online bulletin board – a place for you to pin pictures of things you love and share them with other people. I believe this is what is known as a "Vision Board" in some circles, and you can't just be on Pinterest – you have to request an invitation. The site says you can plan a wedding, redecorate your home, find your style, or save your inspirations. I don't need the Internet to write down things I like, because I actually have a pad and a pencil. Some of the "must see" items on the main page are about how to make a photo family tree – not with my family– and how to make crayon hearts – don't need that either. That's not my Vision Board. My Vision Board is pictures of money, shoes, and Idris Elba or this guy I saw working in Herve Leger on Melrose.

The first time I perused the site I did notice a lot of yummy food items. Then I saw a recipe for a "Baked Egg Boat," which was eggs baked in a delicious crispy crusty baguette, and something called "Pink Lemonade Pound Cake," and quite frankly those things are definitely on my Vision Board. Now I'm thinking about applying to Pinterest and praying I'll get accepted. I didn't know it was a billboard for the food obsessed. I'm not sure what I have to do to be accepted, but I'm working on a Pinterest acceptance "Vision Board" and resume right now while I wait to hear if I'm in. It has pictures of cookies in a garbage disposal and me eating out of it with a fork because, that's the kind of shit that peaks my Pinterest.

It seems there are a lot of things on the web just for women. Case in point: *HuffPost Women*, which seems to be a site dedicated to reminding me how dumb women can be when it comes to men. The site had some terrific/stupid articles, like "The Ten Cities With The Most Sensitive Men" and "Dumped Via Text." I ignored both of these immediately because I don't care where the sensitive men live. Nobody wants to date a crier. *Why not make me a flow chart of where all the assholes are? Oh wait – I can do that one myself -it's called my "contact list."* As for the dumped by text, if you're a woman getting broken up with by a cell phone communication, then you must have asked for it. Either you talk too much when he calls and he couldn't get a word in edgewise, or you picked the wrong man. Try dating down a little - like someone too young to spell or get approved for his own cell phone credit line. This way, he'll have to ditch you in person. Lower your standards, people.

And if you want to add insult to injury, check out *HuffPost 50*. This site promises to be a treasure trove of ideas for someone like me who is the typical 53-year-old. Two of the articles I found intriguing were "How to Get Your Doctor to Love You" and "How to Get Your Grandchild to Stop Lying." I have to say I've never really worried about how to get my doctor to love me. For the most part, I try to focus on how to get him to give me free drugs. Maybe this is what I'm doing wrong. But if someone could figure out how to get people to stop lying to me, that would be a bonus. Where's that article? There was also a fabulous cringe-worthy story called "How to Embrace Your Gray Roots." Listen up, everyone: The people running this website are without a doubt smoking the fattest crack bowl in the history of mankind. There is nothing sexy about gray hair. I will continue to spend money getting rid of my grays, and when it becomes gray pubic hair, I'm calling the police. They must have a division that handles this. Law and Order St. Fu.

None of these articles can help me. I need someone to write a story that tells me how to use the word "foolishness" more or how to kill someone with just my eyes. That would be useful to me. Where's the story about how to turn gas into electricity – and I'm not talking about the kind you get at the pump. Nobody really wants to hear about life after 50. Even the newest shows about this age are produced for the web only, which is ironic because most 50-year-olds only know how to go on Facebook – and then they even screw that up when they write a dumb embarrassing post on your wall because they thought they were sending you a private message. "Hey Heidi – remember when we fucked?" *Umm, yeah. Now my mom knows too. Thanks, Uncle Tim.*

Overall I think this interweb thing may be here to stay. I could be wrong. I've been wrong before. I never thought "Yes Dear" would make it to syndication and haunt me nightly from dozens of cable channels. I am currently addicted to a few fashion blogs, thanks to my very stylish and very fashionably in-touch niece Amy and her equally stylish mother – my sister Wendy. My super-fashionable sister Alison also works in the style business, so I guess you could say all of the women in my family will go broke from purchasing. I am so obsessed with one site in particular, and I use it to get dressed in the morning. I scour through the photos and then pluck something similar from my closet. Or worse, I go out and purchase the item the Blogger tells me I need. So far, I've needed quite a few things. I would tell you the website if I wasn't a selfish bitch – but I am – and I don't need any more people stealing the fashion ideas I'm stealing. We already look like a bunch of "Sex & The City" rejects in LA. There is enough ass- cheek showing on a nightly basis that all of Hollywood is beginning to look like a red-light district.

It's also remarkable how many people are videotaping themselves making instructional videos for how to do stupid or mundane shit no one needs to know how to do and putting it on the web for all to see. There is nothing you can't find out how to do on the Internet. My friend Sharon learned how to install a garbage disposal by watching an instructional video – although I've never been to her house to see it in action, and it could be spewing carrot pulp into her tub right now for all I know. I watched two videos the other day on how to apply mascara and one on how to blow-dry my hair. There are millions of them. I'm thinking about making one for how to put on your shoes, eat oatmeal, and use a pen. I think I'd get a lot of hits. There are a lot of instructional videos on how to use something called Philadelphia Cooking Cream. Barf. What is Philadelphia

Cooking Cream, and who thought it was a good idea to can up something that looks like what you find at the bottom of your tissue during cold and flu season? I saw a commercial for the lumpy, goopy, disgusto cheesy, saucy blech-like mess, and I actually had to look twice because I thought I was watching an "SNL" fake spot. There is no way someone at Kraft was shown this idea and said, "Yes – let's make a can of snot for America!!!" I know these are the same people who brought us Plastic Meat and Cheese Sliced Lunchables and those brilliant 100-calorie packs of anything they can get their hands on, but this new product just looks like beige slime. I guess it must be popular and selling like hot cakes, judging from the hundreds of Betty Homemakers on the internet telling me how they used Flemadelphia Cooking Cream. They had a lot of hits – more than my blog. There was one woman who said, "What do you get when you have plain old chicken breast and Philadelphia Cooking Cream? My very own creation of oven- baked chicken with Philadelphia Cooking Cream surprise!" *Huh? What's the surprise? That you're really a man in a wig in your kitchen?*

Another woman on another video was making something fried with the gunk and pancake mix and said, "How did I come up with this recipe?" Actually I was wondering *why* she came up with this recipe, because she weighed A LOT. Another woman said she was happy to be back in her kitchen, "cooking for the real women of Philadelphia." I guess all you other phony people can just tune out.

Everyone wants to be doing something other than what they're doing – myself included. Just troll around the web, and you'll see ordinary Americans trying to live out their dreams– leaving a legacy of odd digital moments that will survive long after they die. My fifty-something-year-old tax man is in a band. He's been writing songs since I went to see him 15 years ago. He's about to start playing in clubs in LA, and I will be there when he hits the stage. I truly believe that every human being has some creative itch they're trying to scratch. Unfortunately for some, it may involve something we don't really need to see in a video – on the web. I do think the world would be a better place if everyone got to do what they wanted to do – at least once in a while. Dream big. But if that dream is how to make spaghetti with Philadelphia Cooking Cream and clams – please keep that video to yourself. I don't like throwing up while I'm trying to find the "how to put on underpants one leg at a time" video.

There are quite a few self-proclaimed experts on the Internet who tell you how to be the perfect woman. I hate all of these women. Okay, hate is a strong word. I want to murder all of these women – one in particular. I don't want to tell you her name because that would be mean, so let's just say her website rhymes with "Bupcakes and Bashmere". Every day on "Bupcakes and Bashmere," this young, Martha Stewart-like woman tells me a few of her favorite things. Pearl encrusted fingernails for fashion week or chocolate-covered banana bites – the only thing to do with leftover melted chocolate (Trust me, there are other things to do with leftover melted chocolate, like lick it out of the pot you melted it in in the first place because you found some bittersweet cooking chocolate in the back of your fridge). She has traveling tips for what to pack, how to make your own headbands, how to create the perfect updo, and how to make candles in antique teacups. She should post "how to build a bomb" – because she's making my head explode. Every day I try to avoid the site, but every day it pulls me back in and every day it makes me feel like less of a person. *What will she be creating today?* She had a photo of her fabulous new manicure that matched her iPhone case. I don't even have an iPhone case. Well I did, but I lost it. She takes pictures of herself, and her outfits, and her closet, and her jewelry drawers, and all of the creative ways she makes her life chic and fabulous, and I guess the bottom line is, she's making me feel badly about myself because I can't make an airplane out of an old shoe and use it to fly to Fashion Week. I'm pretty sure she can. I guess I could stop being a hater, but I just want to search her name in Google one day and find a picture of her eating something out of a garbage can or falling down in the street drunk or I don't know… Give me something, please, before I crawl into an inferior ball and die of shame!!

I still have my very first laptop computer. It weighs more than my house. I do enjoy the ease with which we can do things these days courtesy of technology, like paying bills or buying shoes or looking up "how to braid your pubic hair," but I feel like we all need to get out of the house more. I love that I can find out anything by simply tapping into a keyboard, but maybe I should just go to a library and read a book. Remember when we had those?

Chapter Sixteen

I'm The Captain Now

Let's face it, if being a woman were easy, everyone would do it. I mean, who would say "no" to a life of fabulous shoes and the ability to change your hair color as often as you change your underwear? We are the lucky ones. And if I knew at 20 what I now know at 53, I could have been President of something – not the United States, because that would have cut way down on my shopping and I don't think the first family Chanukah photo would be acceptable with dogs dressed as kids – but President of something.

Women are our own worst enemies and we need to change that. It's okay if it takes you 50 years to figure out how to love yourself, but you definitely need to figure out how to love other women while you're on your journey of self discovery, because we self doubting, body- dysmorphic bitches need to stick together. And quite frankly, some of you bitches need to stop pissing me off so I can start liking you more. If there's one thing I've come to realize it's that when it comes to the fox hole that is life, I need a fox with a hole to help me survive.

A twenty-something-year old female friend told me recently that she was having trouble making other girlfriends. She's strong, smart, and generally all-around amazing. I told her, "It'll be fine when you're 40. That's when most girls like us stop competing with each other and realize we're better together than apart. And we're

not trying to steal each other's boyfriends, and souls."
Well, most of us. Some girls are lucky enough to have
girlfriends their entire lives – and some of us – well, we
just don't figure it out until later in life that women are
not the enemy. Most women.

I was definitely the enemy once or twice in life, and I
also got stabbed in the front, back, and side along the
way by a few other femmes fatales, but as I get older, I
gain more female friends, and I'm not afraid to say
"goodbye" to the ones who didn't always have my back.
Now, in the second half of my life I'm really trying to
support fellow vagina owners, and the first thing we need
to do is stop pinning all of our hopes and dreams on men.
The second thing we need to do is cancel "The Bachelor"
or, as I like to call it, "Vagina For Sale."

There's a reason there are hardly ever any African
American women on this show. Black girls would not put
up with that shit.

"The Bachelor" is made up of desperate white
women throwing themselves at dopey white men and
having sex with them on national television. Proud
moments, ladies. Don't they know America is on the
other end of that penis? You're making a porn, honey.
Any time I've ever watched the show and the guy says,
"Will you accept this rose?" – I vomit. He's offering her
a flower for her vagina. My vagina deserves a lot more
than a rose. My vagina deserves a car or some jewelry.
In fact, it deserves a car filled with jewelry. I'd definitely
bang The Bachelor on my special one-on-one date if he
gave me that, but I would punch him right in the face if
he handed me a rose.

We also need to band together and stop the nonsense
that is the romantic comedy... or at least the ones that

aren't "When Harry Met Sally." I myself fall for them every time, and I probably have written one or two, but they always end the same – me with a bunch of empty candy wrappers and boxes to things I shouldn't have eaten, believing once again that there are perfect Princes out there. These movie people know how to get us, hook – line – and stinker – aka – the guy who doesn't exist. I mean, the plot lines are pretty much all the same these days. Boy meets Girl. Boy gets Girl. Boy dumps Girl because he's a Moron. Girl takes Boy back anyway. They live happily ever after, or at least until the credit roll is over.

You know why you never see sequels to hugely popular romantic comedies? All the couples are divorced. If we all lived in that sappy existence, we'd run out of insulin. I watched one the other night however that was a full-on slap across the face to women and their friendships. In the movie, Kate Hudson is a hideous self-centered bitch who's about to marry a super hot guy. Her best friend, who shall remain nameless because I happen to know someone she dated in real life and cheated on and I will never forgive her, is the one who introduced Kate to the guy in the first place and blah blah blah the plot line is so heavy and hard to follow, my head hurt and it made figuring out "Inception" a walk in the park. I still have no idea what happened in *that* movie.

Anyway, this chick sleeps with Kate Hudson's fiancé, and the movie tells us this is okay because she really loved him first and Kate Hudson is an annoying cunt anyway (in the movie, people). At some point, I found myself literally screaming at the television. *"Hello??? Every single woman in the world has a best friend who's a cunt, but this does not make it okay to fuck her boyfriend or fiancé.* I will never forgive Angelina Jolie for what she did to Jennifer Aniston. I know it takes two to tango, and she and Brad are clearly meant to be together, but this is a really fucked-up thing to do to another woman. It just is. Now in the movie, this chick gets the guy and Kate gets something every evil bitch needs to become whole and sweet – a baby. Holy shit, I almost blew out my TV. Then in the end, we see a pregnant Kate Hudson running down the street trying to catch yet another guy. What???? By the way, this movie is based on a book that probably sold 12 billion copies while I sit here writing and reading things out loud to my dogs, who do not seem all that impressed, but I'm sorry – me no likey.

For me, one of the hardest things about being a single woman is finding other women I can relate to. I do not want to spend my entire night talking about men or sex. This may have something to do with the fact that I don't have either, which is a heated discussion in itself, but come on ladies, isn't there something else for us to talk about? I'm sorry I just said, "Come on, ladies." Men who are total strangers can get together and instantly bond about sports. They go on and on talking about the teams and players and the runs and the averages and the hits and ohmigod, my head is going to explode. It's as if they actually own them or have some sort of stake in the outcome of a game or a trade or whatever that shit is about. Women do not have this same area of mutual knowledge. We need something. Not men. Not sex. Not even shoes.

We also may need to get rid of the Lifetime Movie Network. My friend Brian says the logo for this channel should be a closed door and the sound of a woman screaming. The entire network seems to be devoted to bad shit happening to women. If you're slightly depressed and watch the Lifetime Movie Network, you will for sure kill yourself by the end of the evening. Last night, the big Saturday night movie was called "Mom, Dad and Her." I'm guessing it was about some hideous woman who stole someone's husband – aka – The Angelina Jolie Story. I couldn't watch it because I was too busy creating the "Criminal Minds" drinking game. This is where you take a shot every time Shemar Moore says the words "baby girl." You'll be shitfaced in ten minutes.

When it comes right down to it, the main difference between men and women is that men can do tricks with their penises that we cannot do with our vaginas. Men treat their penises like toys. They make videos like "Meatspin", "Vacuum Blowjob," and "Origami Penis" and dedicate Broadway shows to it like "Puppetry of the Penis." Even if women could do a play with their vaginas, it would consist of one imitation – a Dolphin – and that's not really worth $700 a ticket. Maybe if we could have more fun with our vaginas, we wouldn't take the damn things so seriously. A little twatfoolery could be good for ladies so that we too could dominate the web with fun movies we make with our girlfriends. We could spend hours together lighting our vagina farts on fire and punching each other in our private parts and laughing.

Someone forwarded me an article about women they thought was the greatest thing they'd ever read. It was written by Andy Rooney. Turns out he had a couple two three things to say about women over 40 – and those things were just as annoying as the reports he used to do when he fiddled with things on his desk and then turned them into four-hour reports about the trouble with paper clips when they stick to the inside of the magnetic holder and how it annoys him. Well, I have a few things to say about what he had to say. His statements are in quotes.

"As I grow in age, I value women who are over 40 most of all. A woman over forty will never wake you in the middle of the night to ask, "What are you thinking?" She doesn't care what you think."

First of all, we should value women of all ages. Not just the ones over 40. Yes, getting to this age by surviving you people – men – is a miracle, but start valuing us from the start and it will get easier as we grow. Second of all, we do care what you think; we've just been programmed to stop asking you because you get mad and say, "Quit asking me if I'm thinking something." Just admit you are thinking something already!

"A woman over 40 knows herself well enough to be assured in who she is, what she is, what she wants, and from whom. Few women past the age of forty give a hoot what you might think about her or what she's doing."

Every person under 40 is becoming who they will be in the future. Men are allowed to be who they want. Powerful, smart, outspoken etc. Women are not. We just wear you down so that by the time we're forty – it's almost acceptable to not give a shit about what you think. But it's also a shame.

"Women over 40 are dignified. They seldom have a screaming match with you at the opera or in the

middle of an expensive restaurant. Of course, if you deserve it, they won't hesitate to shoot you, if they think they can get away with it."

Women under 40 can also be dignified. Especially the ones who figure out how to murder you with no one finding out. Screaming at someone in the middle of an opera is perfectly acceptable if you deserve it. Enough said. Quit trying to quiet us down.

"Older women are generous with praise, often undeserved. They know what it's like to be unappreciated."

No, we just finally figured out how to get stuff from you idiots.

"Women over 40 couldn't care less if you're attracted to her friends because she knows her friends won't betray her."

Actually, she is also secretly hoping that friend will betray her and praying that friend would be willing to give you a blow job, because she's done doing it.

"Women get psychic as they age. You never have to confess your sins to a woman over 40. They always know."

We've always known.

"A woman over 40 looks good wearing bright red lipstick. This is not true of younger women."

Red lipstick looks good on any woman who thinks it looks good on her. Half the battle of life is feeling confident.

"Once you get past a wrinkle or two, a woman over 40 is far sexier than her younger counterpart."

Get past a wrinkle or two? Gee thanks, fat, old, hairy man who probably smelled like fart.

"Older women are forthright and honest. They'll tell you right off if you are a jerk, if you are acting like one! You don't ever have to wonder where you stand with her."

We're simply exhausted from not being listened to for years and we finally don't give a shit what you think. Let her tell you how she really feels without badgering her or breaking up with her when she's young and you'll have a magnificent relationship. Stop trying to change the women you fall in love with so you can rule over them like kings.

In fact – how about everyone backing the fuck up out of my vagina in general and by everyone – I mean men. I'm sorry, but unless you can do the following five things – you don't get a say in anything involving my lady parts.

Wax it. Get up on a table – put your legs in the air – and have someone put hot wax on your scrotum, then rip it off.

Bleed. Spend four days a month shoving cotton carpet rolls inside yourself to stop hemorrhaging after you spend two weeks eating everything in sight.

Bloat. Wake up 15 pounds fatter than when you went to be because you have a hormone imbalance.

Give Birth. Shove a watermelon with knobs out of what feels like your ass.

Be Judged. Have people pay less attention to what you say simply because of who you are.

It's not easy being female, especially when the one thing we have that has any power is constantly under attack or being threatened with new male leadership. I know it's an old cliché, but if men had vaginas, the world would be a very different place. I'm glad men have their own problem in their pants, but maybe God should have just given both sexes boobs. If a Republican had to leave the Vagina Panel because he was lactating and had to pump - at least that would level the playing field.

It's taken me fifty plus years to figure some shit out, but I value being a woman, and at the end of the day I know who I am, I know who I want to be, and I like myself... a lot. I've also learned a few things along the way.

#1 – Celebrate each and every birthday. The bigger the blowout the better. Every day you wake up is a gift. Never forget that. Plus, people give you shit on your birthday. Free shit. If you keep getting candles from friends – change those friends until you get ones who give you shoes.

#2 – Never allow someone else's opinion of you define how you feel about yourself. Bullies all have one thing in common – fear. They're afraid you'll find out who they are, and so they strike first. The only person who should define you – is you. And stop being so hard on yourself. You're probably smarter than everyone you know. How do I know? You're reading my book. You're a fucking genius.

#3 – Be open-minded. You never know where you'll find magic. Just go to a reputable psychic. HaHaHaHa. I'm kidding. There's no such thing dummy.

#4 – Life will not be perfect if you find a mate. Don't look for your other half – find someone who is already whole. You already are your own soul mate. Try dating yourself. You already know what you like and there's no chance you'll date rape yourself.

#5 – Accept your parents. They gave you life. Be kind to the elderly. They know stuff. Like where to get a really good pool noodle.

#6 – Eat until you're 40. After that, it all goes to shit.

#7 – Menopause sucks. The end.

#8 – Plastic surgery is not the answer. Cake is. Sometimes you need to fix the inside.

#9 – Being a drunken idiot is a waste of time. Everything in moderation. Except shoes.

#10 - Every girl needs a gay. Or two.

#11 – A dog will eat your poop and then lick your face. You won't care.

#12 – Think before you ink. Or at least stay away from the face.

#13 – You'll always want what you can't have. It's okay. Somebody somewhere is jealous of what you have. You win.

#14 – A good handyman is better than a husband. If you can combine them – you're way up in the game of life.

#15 – Stay plugged in. It will keep you young.

Take ownership of your life, and embrace the woman you are. She's all you've got. My friend Brian said that sounds like a perfume ad. I told him to fuck off. Now if you'll excuse me, I need to go buy some shoes.

About the Author:

Heidi Clements is an Executive Producer and writer on the ABC Family sitcom "Baby Daddy." She is addicted to good shoes and bad cake. She lives in Los Angeles with her three dogs, her debt, and the judgment of others. Thankfully it's a pretty big house.